CW00404200

TRANSACTIONS of DESIRE

Edited by
Omar Kholeif
& Sarah Perks

CONTENTS

INTRODUCTION

What does it mean to love, to fall in love, to be loved?
That prickle on your nose, that itch in your bum, those beads of sweat that develop under your armpits?
This is the sexual life of you and me and everyone we know.
A child is born.
Memories will flood.
The relation between what we see and what we feel – fuzz.
Self-awareness, for a little while anyway
Admiration, fear, love, self-loathing?
Aspiration: substitution for prostitution
An orgy inside your head
The obsessions of the past, the thrill of youth
They have made a movie of you:
That first cigarette
The first time you had goosebumps
The first time you recoiled from touch
Fingers intertwining
Under the tree, the stars, the astroplane
Seeing seething desire. It is invisible.
The child looks and recognises love, before it can even speak.

OMAR KHOLEIF & SARAH PERKS
April 2015

The Heart is Deceitful Above All Things

SARAH PERKS

ROXY AND REBECCA
463 HENNESSY ROAD
CAUSEWAY BAY
HONG KONG
4:00 AM

Babe, are you awake?

Not really, what's up?

I think we need to talk? Bex?

Now?

Yes.

I'm so tired and aching from moving. I don't know how we got all those boxes up the stairs. Why doesn't the lift go from the bottom?

It's an old building; it's quaint … can we talk for a minute please?

Okay, baby, talk.

I don't think we should have moved in together.

Roxy! What are you saying? Why are you saying this now?

I don't know. I just haven't got to sleep. I've just got this overwhelming feeling that I made the wrong decision. I've been lying here for hours and I can't lie here any longer. I don't know why, I just think … I can't see us here together.

Did we pick the wrong apartment? Should we have moved to the one in Kennedy Town instead? Oh god I'm so sorry.

No, it's not the apartment, it's us. I mean … I mean I can't see us together. Now. Or tomorrow. God I sound terrible and cheesy I know, I just don't know how to say this Bex, I'm sorry.

You remember the other night at the fortune-teller near Temple Street?

I told you not to do that Roxy.

It wasn't what he said, but it started then. This sneaking feeling that I needed to run, get out, that I'm in some way missing something.

I don't really know what I can say Rox. I'm half asleep. We've just moved into this place here and after not even one night, you want to go?

The teller said that big changes were coming, later this year. I don't believe him but the thought of everything staying the same was somehow worse. Shit, I'm sorry Rebecca … Bex … I can't say this, I can't say how I feel, but I think I'm going to have to go.

Where have you been Rox? You went for an hour.

Just walked around.

What are you going to do? I love you. I don't understand this. I want us to go to sleep, get up, get the place tidy, buy some stuff, I was gonna say maybe go out later.

I'm going to sort my boxes out, get some stuff and go to Jo's.

What? Roxy, what's going on, I don't understand any of this? I don't know what you want me to do.

Do you want breakfast? Some eggs? Coffee? Roxy?

Are you going to talk to me? Or just keep moving the same things around.

It's too early to go yet … no one is awake.

It's a bit too early to go full stop I think.

There's no need to be like that Bex.

Really? What exactly should I be like? We've been going out for two years and you ask me if I want us to live together and I say yes and then not even a day later you change your mind! Is this about Zoe? Has something gone on between you?

No, I don't know why you said that. Bex, I've never thought about her. Why do you say that?

That day we were at Kim's meal and you said …

Don't bring that up again.

I really love you Roxy you know, I don't know what I'm going to do now. I just don't know.

I'll pay the rent for a while.

Fuck you.

Well I will. I should do.

Are we still going to see each other?

Probably best if we don't for a while. I need some space.

Fuck you again.

I know you're upset.

You have no idea.

I'm sorry.

It's not me, it's you, yeah?

Something like that. I don't know why things just end.

Cos you want them too. Cos you don't want to work at it anymore.

I guess.

I can't.

What Bex?

Guess your reasons. Just go, I hate this. I really fucking hate this. You'll be back.

What's that? What did you drop Bex?

My Yoda alarm clock.

It's horrible.

I like it.

I don't know why you would.

Like you say, some things are hard to explain. You said it.

Sort of. Are you going to be okay if I go now?

Yes. No. What does it matter?

I still love you.

Fuck you.

ROB AND FREYA
THE BREAKFAST CLUB
SHOREDITCH
LONDON
8:00 PM

Sorry I'm late. So sorry, I just … the overground … it's like, busy.

Sit down gorgeous, I ordered some stuff ahead. Some pickles too.

My favourite.

I know. And some mojitos.

I so love you, thank you Rob. Just gotta run to the loo, be back asap.

So how's your day?

Busy. Really busy. Haven't stopped. Had to file two articles and upload some stuff. You?

Just went to the gym and a bit of shopping.

Clothes?

No I mean food, Freya!

Did you see the FB invite from Tim?

Yeah, that looks amazing, shall we go?

When is it again?

Week on Saturday.

Okay great.

Did you see that woman over there? I'm sure she was in Dalston at that café place the other day.

OTO?

Yeah. She has weird light pink hair. Probably done at Bleach. On the bus before from there I saw someone with the green colour. Sounds bad, but looks quite good.

I thought you just came from home? On the overground?

Oh, no, I had to pop via Dalston just to like, get something.

What?

I mean see someone. Tim.

Why?

Just wanted his opinion. He was really helpful actually … he helped me.

He's not there.

Where?

Dalston.

He was.

Just before you got here, when I saw his event, I also saw he'd gone to the coast for the day. Posting that they were waiting for sundowners. You didn't go to see Tim. So what were you doing?

I don't know.

You don't know?

I … I went to see Joe.

Can I have a glass of tap water with this? I'll order mains later. Thanks.

What the hell were you doing with Joe? You know how I feel about him. Freya, look at me. Why are you crying?

Is there something going on Freya?

I wanted to tell you sooner.

Tell … what?

I'm sorry; I'm seeing Joe again. I know why we broke

up. I know why we're together. But he just didn't leave me alone and I know it's stupid but I just love him, and I can't keep away from him. And I know he's not you, and you're the one I should be with, but …

What the hell? Are you drunk? Why are you telling me this? Is this because of Tuesday night?

No no no.

You know that was just a mistake, and I couldn't be there for you, and I said I was sorry.

So why now?

What do you mean Rob?

Why are you telling me this? You could have just said, look the last few months have been amazing, but I couldn't get over my ex and it's best we spilt up before anything happens.

Sorry. I didn't intend for this.

What exactly did you intend then?

I wanted to fall in love with you. I did. I gotta go to the loo.

There's something else, Rob.

I don't know if I want to talk here. Do you want to walk?

No, I just wanted to tell you first. Before you hear from someone else.

I don't think I can stay here.

It's …

I mean it, I have to go.

Wait! Joe asked me … he asked me …

Message me. I don't think I want to know right now. I think I best just leave.

He asked me to marry him. He asked me and I

said …
Can I have the cheque?

Why don't you want to know?
I think you know why. You let me, you let me … you let me carry on for months and now you say you are …
I'm sorry, I really am. I really …
Never mind.

Keep the change. I'll not see you at Tim's birthday. I'll see you around.

CARLOS AND ANTHONY
DOGS: PICKLE AND YODA
SILVERLAKE RESERVOIR
LOS ANGELES
12:00 PM

Hey Carlos, how's Yoda? He's looking lively today.
I didn't get chance to walk him yesterday so he's really ready for this!
Pickle is a bit feisty too. But then he always is, check his tail go!
They love their walks together!
It's becoming a habit for sure.
This time of year is great, not too hot.

Did you hear about Suzie?
Yeah I thought her gig sounded fab. She's really going places.
Do you want some of this soda?
Yeah thanks.
Does Pickle want a treat?

Sure, thanks. If she stops barking a minute. Pickle!

Do you think they love each other?

Who?

Yoda and Pickles!

Oh, yeah, I know they do, look at them chase each other!

How do you know they do?

You can just tell with dogs. They are so comfortable with each other. Or they take an instant dislike and bark bark growl, haha.

Or do they just take their cue from their owners? If their owners like each other?

No! Phil and Seb still have to separate their dogs. They can't leave them in the same room. They love each other but their dogs are like, no way.

I've always wondered about Phil and Seb though, they have so little in common. I don't really know them though, just friends of Suzie's. Seem always a bit distant with each other.

They just not touchy feely but they crazy in love for sure.

How do you know?

I seen them chasing each other! Butt sniffing and tail wagging!

Are you having a summer holiday this year?

I hope so, I can't really plan. Crazy schedule. I'm not sure where I'll be. Love to get away though, maybe just drive up the coast.

Malibu?

Ha, no, further, maybe San Fran. Do some wine trails.

That would be so amazing. I want to do that. No real plan, stop at different places, drink a ton of Merlot or something.

Actually I don't really drink, but Yoda loves it up there. I'll maybe get a gang together. You should come along Carlos?

Love to.

Pickles just totally jumped that big dog. The grey one. I'm so embarrassed; he should know he is so out of his league.

Yoda covered his eyes.

Ha! He clever that dog. Like his Daddy!

My eyes are shut most of the time. Or wearing shades at least. Oh shit, I think they fell out of my pocket! I took them off to get the poop.

Let's go back round and see?

You sure, it'll take longer.

No worries, I'm enjoying this, let's walk back and then back again!

Yey.

Found them!

You look so hot in those. I really want some new glasses.

So you can look as hot as me?

Hotter.

I got these in Hong Kong, I don't think you can buy them here anyway.

Well I'm glad you didn't lose them for sure.

Me too.

Do you lose much stuff?

Not really.

Me too. I never really lose anything.

Have you seen Yoda's ball?

He just had it!

I know but now it's totally like vanished. Yoda! Where you ball?

I thought you didn't lose anything!

Not me, Yoda! YODA! WHERE YOU BALL?

Why did you call him Yoda?

I didn't, Andrew did. Stupid *Star Wars* fan.

Oh yes, I remember the story. He didn't look enough like Luke!

Luke is a stupid name for a dog.

Totally.

I gotta like get back soon actually, I just remembered a deadline.

Do you wanna get together for a drink?

Yeah sure, we only ever walk!

How about Akbar? Next weekend?

Do you mean Andrew and Pablo too?

I was kind of thinking just us?

Okay, cool. Let's do it Saturday.

Great, I might be having a BBQ Sunday too. Bring Yoda. Not to Akbar's though.

Obvs.

Do you think Pablo will mind?

I don't know. We're just hanging out yes?

Yes. I look forward!

Me too.

Bye Pickles!

Bye Yoda!

Bye you!

361

Douglas Coupland

First, let me tell you who I am. I'm Sharon Firth and I was an elementary school teacher in Vancouver, Washington – not the Canadian Vancouver – the other Vancouver across the Columbia River from Portland, Oregon, and I really liked teaching younger kids. Younger kids are so sweet, but I will add that at thirteen the girls turn into bitches and when I look at their little heads all I can see in the classroom is shoplifted mascara and thought balloons filled with very cruel nicknames for me – or whoever got stuck teaching them. Boys become sulking monsters at fifteen, and that's easier to handle. So, yes, I got to teach the young kids, and it really was like teaching angels, but I'm also very aware that it is dangerous to confuse angels with children, and this is my tale.

It was in late October, 1975.

It was just past three and class had gotten out for

the day. Most of the kids had gathered their things and left, then there were a few stragglers, and then there was quiet, and when I looked up there was one student sitting calmly in his chair, Greg Cushing, the sweetest little guy ever, little brown curls and never any sass. He was twelve.

'Greg, sweetie? You're not leaving?'

'I'm not Greg.'

'Greg, I've got papers to mark, and I don't have time for games. Come on now, scoot. Get home. Your Mama's waiting for you.'

'I'm not Greg.'

I decided to go along with it. 'So then, if you're not Greg, who might you be?'

'I don't have a name. Not the way you think of names. I guess you'd call it more of a number than a name.'

'Okay ...'

'This is Greg's body. I've hijacked it. He's not here right now. Greg is in storage.'

'Greg, sweetie, you're scaring me.'

'I guess you're not listening to me ... *Sharon*. If you want to call me a name, call me 361.'

That's when I understood it was real. It doesn't take much. Greg wasn't there.

I exhaled, and sat back in my chair to collect my thoughts. It was a rainy day already and getting dark out, even at 3:30 PM. I wanted to run out of the room, and badly, but how could I?

'Okay 361, tell me something that would confirm to me you are indeed alien.'

'Very well. You're lesbian but you're not coping with it, and the stress of maintaining a heterosexual façade is causing you to overeat and gain weight. You think nobody knows, but there's always chatter in the staffroom. And in any event, suppressing your identity is making you profoundly unhappy. You've contemplated leaving teaching and leaving Vancouver, but you have a cowardly streak and it will probably get the better of you. It will set you up for a lifetime of pain and regret.'

I stood up and stared at him. I walked over – I didn't even look to see if the doors were open or if anyone was looking – and I slapped him hard on the face. 'How dare you.'

'A slap. How cliché, Sharon. As if a slap is going to make the truth go away. Here, while you're at it, why don't you kick Greg's body and damage it – give it scars. Give it something to make his Mama want to take you to court.'

I was terrified. I didn't know what to do.

'Sit down,' said 361. 'I'm not here to hurt you.'

I slumped down and sat in the seat of the desk beside him. The chair was tiny. I felt fat. And 361 was indeed correct in everything he had said about me.

'Good,' he said, 'I think I've got your attention.'

'Where do you come from?'

'Excuse me?'

'Where do you come from? Some other planet? Why are you on Earth?'

'You've been watching too much late night TV, Sharon. If I'm alien, it's only in personality.'

I could feel myself sweating. My ears were buzzing. I don't know what I was … maybe what it feels like if a panther walked into the room and was sniffing around while I sat there hoping I didn't smell like panther chow.

'I can see you need time to think over my brief visit, Sharon. To prove to you I'm legitimate, I'll give you a list of things that are going to happen in the world over the next week.'

'What?'

'Just stop and listen. Today, October 27th, a man in Ottawa, Canada killed five people in a high school and then shot himself. You just haven't heard about it yet. Also today, Rex Stout, an American detective novel writer died. Tomorrow, Georges Carpentier, a French boxer, will die. On the 29th, President Ford will announce that he will veto any legislation for a federal bailout of New York City. The cover of the *New York Daily News* the next day will read, 'Ford to City: Drop Dead.' That same day, Juan Carlos the First of Spain will become acting head of state after dictator Francisco Franco concedes he is too ill to govern. Also, a Yugoslavian airliner will crash while attempting to land in Prague and all seventy two people on board will die.'

'How do you ... ?'

'Shush. I'll see you again same time next week. Goodbye Sharon.'

Greg's – *361's* – head slumped and then suddenly it was Greg there, no mistaking it, and seeing me there with an astonished face quite reasonably freaked him out.

'Miss Firth? Wait – what happened? Where is everyone? Why are you here? Am I in trouble?'

I sucked in breath. 'Sweetie, I think you have a cold. You'd better go home to your Mama.'

'So I'm not in trouble or anything?'

'You? Greg, you don't have a troubled bone in your

body. No go home. Scoot.'

'Bye Miss Firth.'

I really don't know what I thought. Trickery? Demonic possession? Blackmail? I mean … it was simply too mind-blowing to even remotely try to explain to anybody. I couldn't phone my family or my friend Donna because … how could I even begin to ex …

… And then Gerald Ford really *did* tell New York City to screw off – and then Franco *did* concede power – and then the airliner *did* crash. After that I didn't sleep. I had to get through the weekend and not go crazy.

Come Monday, I think the stress was showing. Miss Milne in the staff room offered me Midol, and I could tell I wasn't making a very good show of things. I blew it off as 'Mondayitis' and got a few laughs and then I walked into the classroom to teach. I had to have been on some form of autopilot because all I remember of the day was parroting math lessons, making construction paper chains and trying not to stare at Greg Cushing.

Classes finally ended and students left, and of course, Greg was sitting there.

'Greg?'

'No Sharon. It's not Greg.'

'361. Hello.'

'It's not a very exciting week coming up, Sharon. I wish I could tell you more exciting news but the news is what it is.'

'Why are you speaking to me? How many of you are there?'

'How *many?* That's an odd question that, for various reasons, can't be answered. Let's just say not very many.'

'So again, why are you reaching out to me?'

'Stop this, Sharon. You're being a bore.'

Then 361 went quiet and Greg's body froze, like he was rewinding or something, and then he said:

> We are your friends.

But with this he was no longer using Greg's voice. Something new was speaking and it had a mechanical sound.

'How do I know that?'

> Because we have taken the time to learn about you, assess your life, and develop the choices you can now take to ensure the remainder of your life goes unwasted.

I decided to be tough. 'What would those choices be, then?'

> Leave this Vancouver and go to the other Vancouver. Stop teaching and start making objects with your hands. We recommend metal at the scale of jewelry. That will then make you comfortable within a lesbian existence, and from that you will meet someone who will stick with you until you die.

'Who the hell are you to be telling me what to do with my life?'

We wish you to activate what will most likely be your last chance at what you call happiness.

There was a knock on the door. Ed Jarvis, the Phys-Ed coach, kind of a goofball. 'Am I interrupting anything?'

361 and I turned into the picture of sunshine and happiness. 'Just a bit of detention and some math homework, Ed. Everything okay?'

Ed looked understandably suspicious. 'I came to drop off the unused UNICEF boxes from last week.'

'Oh right. Just put them there by the pencil sharpener. Thanks Ed.'

'No problem.' He dropped the boxes off and left.

361 returned to his normal voice and told me, 'Don't worry about your janitor spreading rumors. Ed steals underwear from his apartment building's drying machines. Just mention that and he'll be quiet.'

'Jesus, what am I in for here?'

'Here is your news for the next week, Sharon. Tomorrow Fidel Castro will order 6,500 troops to Angola. On Wednesday an English rock band called the Sex Pistols will play their first performance at a London art school. On Friday a vapor cloud release in a Dutch petroleum cracking facility in the town of Geleen will kill fourteen people and injure 109. Also on Friday, Patricia Hearst will be declared fit to stand trial. That's it, I'm afraid. All in all, an incredibly boring week. Goodbye Sharon.'

And then 361 was gone.

What would you do in a case like this? What would anyone do? I was certainly not dashing off to a church

… and I wasn't going to go run to a shrink. I actually ought to have gone to Donna's brother who dealt weed from the back of his bakery, but I didn't.

And I looked at my life.

361 was absolutely correct. Who was I fooling? I'd dated a few guys in high school but I might as well have been dating cardboard boxes; there was no sexual anything there, and my few forays went nowhere. At the same time it seemed like gay guys were suddenly in the news growing moustaches and having endless sex and there was all this new disco music, and it didn't seem like there was much for a gay woman – certainly not in Vancouver, Washington, more or less a blue collar suburb of Portland. I'd tried meeting gals locally but I have no gaydar or whatever it is you need.

I was lonely. Having to maintain a normal face for the world was taking its toll: *Are you seeing anyone new? Let me help you meet just the right guy* … So, 361 and – whatever the hell he was, he nailed my life, and that was humiliating.

And of course, everything he said would happen that week happened, and come Monday I wasn't so much nervous as I was excited. Miss Milne (she of the Midol) said, 'Aren't you full of beans today?' I giggled nervously – as if she could ever imagine what was happening. All day long, it was the most I could do to contain my excitement and after class ended, for some reason the kids were dawdling that day and I had to almost bark to get them out of the room.

Greg's body sat there waiting for me. 'Hello Miss Firth.'

'Hello 361.'

'I'm hoping by now you understand my authenticity.'

'Yes, I do. So – you're obviously here for a reason: you want me to be happy. Well that's fine and all, but why me? Are there millions of 361s out there going around telling people how to be happy?'

'No, Sharon. You're almost unique.'

'Me? Unique? How? And how does that help you?'

'Your body's cells contain the CCR5-Δ32 variant protein. They lack both CCR5 and CXCR4 receptors on their surfaces, and thus confer you with resistance to a broad range of viruses and their variants.'

'I have no idea what you just said.'

'I am currently inhabiting the body of Gregory, and Gregory is gay.'

'What? He's twelve.'

'Have it your way. He *will* be gay, then.'

'What does that have to do with anything?'

'The virus that will kill him will be one that targets gay men and it will target and kill Greg.'

'What the ... ? How is that even biologically possible? Wait. Don't even ... What does this have to do with me?'

'Greg is doomed. You need to see what's at stake if you don't follow my advice.'

'I'll just give him some of my blood if I'm a living cure.'

'It doesn't work that way. Are you going to knock on his parents' front door and say, "Hello, I'm Sharon and I'd like to give your son some of my bone marrow"? You also have, Sharon, another protein mutation which is important in the year 2018.'

'Who does that one target?'

'Almost everyone, except a few people like you who have another specific protein mutation.'

'If you're so smart, why don't you just club me on the

head and freeze me or something?'

'We would if we could, Sharon, but it doesn't work that way. Channelling Greg here is about the best we can do. And besides, we need you alive.'

'Do you have any idea how creepy you sound?'

'Creepy as sex between two women?'

I whacked Greg/361 across the face then heard a voice, Ed's, behind me.

'What the hell do you think you're doing there, Sharon?'

My face was flushed red. 'Nothing. Mind your own business, Ed. Go steal some panties from your basement dryer.'

The blood drained from Ed's face. What had I done? He stared for a few moments then closed the door and walked away. 'I shouldn't have said that.'

'Not to worry, Sharon, he won't blab.'

I was winded. 'So then what happens next?' I asked. 'Do we meet every Monday from now on?'

'No. You'll hear from me again, but not through Greg.'

'When will that be?'

'Soon enough. It's very difficult for us ... for *me* to do this, Sharon. I'm at the end of my time here. Remember my life advice and take it as quickly as possible. Goodbye.'

It took a minute for Greg to return, during which time I went back to my desk at the front and pretended nothing had happened. When he came to he looked at me. 'Is this a ... detention?'

'No, sweetie, I think you just took a quick nap.'

'Oh. Okay.' Poor doomed Greg got up and left the classroom.

I walked down the hallway and looked outside. It was pouring rain out and the Columbia River was swollen. In a blur I got into my little Datsun and drove home, a small bungalow I got a rental deal on from a friend of my father. I went into the kitchen, stared inside the fridge and poured myself a glass of milk, a reflex whenever I get worried that stemmed from a hygiene class slideshow on the perils of osteoporosis in women.

I put the glass down on the counter and turned around. Ed was standing there, and his eyes were focusing hard on me. 'I don't want to be doing this Sharon.'

I knew what he meant. 'Don't Ed. This is a dumb idea.'

'How did you know?'

'About the underwear? Ed, it doesn't matter.'

'Tell me!'

I made up a lie. 'My girlfriend lives in your building.'

'What's her name?'

I had no idea how big Ed's building was, so I tried to pick as common a name as I could. 'Susan.'

'Her?'

Thank God I'd hit a nail on the head. 'Yes, but she only told me because she knows we work in the same place. She thinks it's funny. But it's your secret, Ed. We won't tell anyone.'

'I can't let that be the case, Sharon.' He took one step toward me.

I tried to slam open the fridge door as a barrier but he pounced too quickly. He put a rope around my neck and I was almost instantly unconscious, but I didn't die. Instead I went into a coma where I am now, and I feel very stupid indeed. Obviously 361, that bastard, was smart enough to see the future, and he engineered the whole Ed fiasco to keep me alive yet immobilised.

And so here I am now. I don't know what the date is or what time of day it is, but I know that my body has become the equivalent of a working farm. Almost daily someone's removing eggs or taking tissue or marrow samples and I suppose I don't mind. I do feel sorry for Greg. He must be long dead by now, and judging by a recent increase in marrow harvesting, I suppose we must be getting closer to the year 2018.

My Love Don't Cost a Thing

ANDREW DURBIN

I purchase two small domestic palms and place them in opposite corners of my bedroom. I don't get much sunlight in the room, but the woman who sold them to me assures me they will be fine because palms like these grow in the dark. She doesn't sell pots large enough to replace the plastic ones they come in so I set them on top of old plates in case they leak, which they often do when I water them. In two weeks, the one in the far corner – where the most sunlight hits the room – starts to wilt, its stalks brown until eventually it collapses in a heap. Gnats gather and bob in the air over its dying body, circling the palm in the concerted manner of a ritual. I wave them away and switch it with the other palm in the room, which was doing fine, though not exactly thriving, and trim all the dead branches of the dying one until it is a third of its original size. The dying plant doesn't come back as I expect it to and the healthy palm wilts with it, finally falling over like the other. I move them both into the kitchen, which is filled with direct sunlight all day, and water them with Miracle-Gro purchased from the same woman who sold me the palms. After a few days the move seems to kill them both. I drag them separately to the curbside of my apartment building, where within a week they both rise up and sprout new, deeply green fronds, rotating toward the sunlight with new life. Someone picks them up before I can bring them back in, and they're gone. Blow up the law, Hélène Cixous writes. Cops define the era. Sit at the café. There is a gym close to here. Dating app. Get together. Go alone. Mood. The problem begins with you, he says. The problem, and the conditions that allow it to be identified as such, suggest that your role in it is essential and that all of this could be avoided were you to leave. I leave. I tell him that the book is called *A Fire in the Belly*. It's by C. Carr. He asks why I said Emily. I never said Emily, I tell him as the subway comes to a full stop in the tunnel. Generationally speaking nothing has changed except the coordinates by which we locate the landscape of our politics – or the politics of landscape. Explicate from the use of those resources a future. Upstate the protest begins. Upstate I sit at a dinner in a yard flushed with berry bushes and discuss the MTA's surprise budget surplus. Every surplus results from an illusory economy seeking to absorb you within it. During a march across the Williamsburg Bridge in solidarity with Ferguson, Missouri, where Mike Brown's killer had been let off the hook, a poet named Eric Linsker is arrested by police and charged with punching an officer. He has a bag of hammers with him. The finger episode, by which I mean the party where you stuck your finger in my ass and made someone else smell it, a gesture that reduced me almost to tears, still keeps me up some nights. The year in destruction, the year of the sheep, the year of those fireworks, the year of the palms, the year of email, the year of soap, the year of the alley, the year of Anicka Yi's *You Can Call Me F* at the Kitchen, the year of F, the year of the refrigerator, the year of a dead father, the year of the text message, the year of address, the year in passing. The fake human skull is wrapped in Saran wrap and sits on a pile of other skulls like it. The yellow plastic makes it look 'real', or at least aged to a semblance of reality I find uncanny, a public token in cheap homage to time, and when I pass it, I stop to take a picture with my iPhone and send it to my friend. When he receives it he writes back:

What is it?

I respond that it's a fake skull on St Mark's. He begins to respond, the small iMessage bubble floating up to indicate that he's typing, but after a few seconds it disappears and he never responds. I think to buy the skull but decide against it. Cancel that.

Romantic poetry didn't know what it was missing. At Kennedy Airport, I take a seat near a man wearing shredded jeans and a plaid shirt over a sweat-stained white tee. With his hiking backpack leaned up against the smoked glass wall next to him, he looks like he's just walked across the country, evidence of a relationship to 'nature' that might be truer or deeper than mine. I write this down in a notebook thinking I could use it later: 'Is nature true or deep?' Reification of the sublime in his and all those bodies walking about, the airport radio plays Taylor Swift, tuned to all dreams of metropolitan space extorted by global capital for the purpose of ubiquitous homogeneity come true, Welcome to New York, Taylor sings, 'It's been waiting for you,' finally risen to the occasion of a world not hers and yet she self-proclaims her kingdom of the very newly saved, the flight attendants circle the smooth floor and the hiker sighs after what must have been a long trip. I secretly take a photo of him with my iPhone, but the flash goes off and he notices me. He shakes his head, grinding his square jaw, but doesn't say anything and looks away. I'm grateful he doesn't confront me so I continue to survey, a little more carefully. He's poring over a water-damaged journal in which he wrote several formal poems, maybe even sonnets, in an unreadable cursive. Poetry really is everywhere. For something to be everywhere it must now be online. Conveniently, poetry is all over the internet because the web itself achieves a kind of poetry, rendering most online bodies poetic machines and thereby enacting in the proliferation of that messy language that illimitable sense of a socialised network of busy intersections pervading all discourses, especially critical ones, infusing most things written and said with an enhanced vitality, all of it glowing on screens scattered across much of the planet. Or have I been lied to? He closes the notebook when his boarding class is called, pulling up his backpack and slinging it over his shoulder as he crosses the crowd clustered at the narrow gate, slipping into it with an ease that suddenly makes me miss him. I forget the feeling once my class is called and I board a jet to Switzerland. Later, over the north Atlantic, I wake up at 4:00 AM East Coast time to see out my window a curvature of gray and blue, bent by a watery, alien light that resembles the flush of the dish water as it finally drains out of the sink. There can be no alien or otherworldly light on earth despite any claims that might attempt to release us into some greater fiction. I felt alone and the flight, on its way to Zurich, was mostly empty. I have not always been careful. I have been tricked into cheap flights, a bot has asked me if I wanted to be friends on Facebook and I have accepted its request, I've opened an email from an acquaintance with a phishing Google doc attached, I've made dumb admissions of fleeting passwords to scammy sites, unlocked accounts for strangers, signed up for porn only to realise it was a tricky financial ruse, and accidentally frozen my Chase card in Chicago when I withdrew $200 for drugs at a goth club. Quinine water once spilled over my laptop in Bushwick, destroying the hard drive, which I hadn't backed up. Later, the gentle acceleration of a plane that puts everyone around to sleep but leaves me awake and jittery bucked my next computer out of my lap and onto the floor, breaking it, and again I hadn't backed anything up. Nothing compares 2 the hike that overlooks LA, nothing compares 2 losing all those useless files, and nothing compares 2 reading Ben's book about debt at Kennedy, where I focused on his interest in the documentary procedures of commerce and our participation in the various markets we rely on, including – and especially – the 'job market'. I've never kept a job for very long, the preconditions of employment (dedication) being so nearly impossible as to abstract every morning to a timeless, flat plane of actions I can't make any sense of, brushing my teeth and putting on my clothes, maybe jerking off while staring at my face in the mirror, drinking orange juice or coffee, eating a banana, all of it seemingly out of order (or finally pledged to a disorder that overrides the desire to put myself together again), until I'm late and too often late and I'm encouraged to look for a job elsewhere. Regardless of my disinterest in definitive employment the pernicious logic of the market still wields its heavy and not so beautiful power over me and everyone else, despite all efforts to debunk it. Pleasures do not accrue with accomplishing any task: your boss is lying to you. I imagine the hiker graduated college and went for a walk, deciding he wouldn't come back. Poems in the cursive of joblessness. To be unemployed is nature.

We live in a joyous age. By which I mean all is available to us. While life, under the imperative to enjoy the self-annihilating transmission of our bodies elsewhere as we conform to it, remains cryptic in its universal demand that we rapidly cycle through all that we adore, all the time, its moments of clarity are just as preciously encoded into the bouts of good feeling that mark these times, as are its moments of obscurity too. On Facebook, I have recently noticed a series of viral, click-bait posts with headlines that assure us we 'won't believe' what we'll see if we click on the link. This woman came home to an intruder in her house. You won't believe what happened next. This man found a sick dog near his house. What he did next will shock you. These posts often lead to nothing or nothing consequential, just other websites that lead to other websites, stupid videos, or ads, ads for ab work outs and coupons for groceries and cheap flights to China, you won't believe what Obama isn't telling you, you will be shocked at this simple trick, I have noticed you, I have noticed you are very interested in cheap air fare, including trips to London, Paris and Beijing. I look up the cost of a flight to Beijing, a city I've always wanted to visit, where my mother went years ago and said was so unbelievable she could not really explain what it was like in any way that my sister and I could understand. Only that she liked it and that we would some day go there and like it too. The airfare site loads Beijing's prices, reasonable as you'd imagine on travelocity.com, the name of which has always been oddly suggestive of some transcendent escape of any present moment, hunched over a laptop or on my phone on the J, in its argument that travel might be a function of speed, only, per usual, the site has trouble loading the good deals it promised and so I give up, head out to a party on a Chinatown roof. Vape terror of heights, vape the feeling it draws out from your stomach and through your asshole as you later approach the ledge of the roof when you're a little too drunk to socialise. Vape those curious hours, swallow them, make eye contact with a dozen boys across the dark roof, lean against the wall while Anton, who's out of money, explains how he came to New York only six months ago and now works in a Japanese stationery store in Chelsea called Muji. He's gotten a little lost since his girlfriend left him and moved to Paris. Listening to him talk about the literal and figurative ocean that separates them is similar to the feeling I get when listening to Prince's Nothing Compares 2 U. In Prince's original version of the song, the lyrics divide between a male and a female speaker, suggesting at least in the reciprocal confusion of longing that they might at last be some day reunited. Like at least they know they are linked together in mutual song. Without changing the lyrics but singing both parts of the song by herself, Sinéad O'Connor, whose version is perhaps more famous, eliminates the lover and shifts that role to us, turning to face the camera in her music video, turning to us, across the unbridgeable gulf split by the screen that divides us, to confer the impossible weight of absence on us. Like it's easy, but also such a burden that I'm overwhelmed to the point I seldom finish watching the video, switch back to travelocity.com, and dream of elsewhere. Earlier, Anton and I had gone through Washington Square Park, sat in the grass for a few hours, and then went our opposite ways home, only to meet up by accident later at the party in Chinatown. We watched jocks throw a ball back and forth in the grass. One of the jocks kept shouting, 'Hit me' several times as his partner waited for the crowd to clear a space for them, impatient to keep the game going, a crowd so densely invested with libidinal drive that it never really divided; or in its temporary incoherence it subdivided briefly until it formed elsewhere, between others. 'Hit me,' they shouted, and then we left. Prince and Rosie become elsewhere while in the spring that overwhelms them the park's tulips bend toward the light. As it turns out, all the flowers in the backyard have not died as Prince and Sinéad said they did. Rather they have situated themselves in the colours that stream toward their sites of radical incoherence, flushed in the afternoon, a place I can never really find, but nevertheless continue to seek. It is sufficient and dense, but must end – or never exist

– in the consummate declaration of an additional end to the present configuration of the afternoon that encircles me. Later on the roof, I vaped under the World Trade. At nine stories up the space between the ground and me was entirely 'poetic': vertical toward the summer night's clouds, the city fixed itself into it. Backgrounded by Nothing Compares 2 U and it's the world. Nothing Compares 2 U and the slow feeling of its subtlety extracts from me a secondary belonging to whatever sky that relents finally to sunrise but differs in almost no way from sunset. Exalt that dumb feeling or else its precious logic collapses in crassly romantic self-possession. Manifest nihilism in the body, summer is the shittiest time for looking cute. Winter, too. Leaning in, Anton whispers to me that I 'have time' when I tell him I'm so tired of having to work, but I'm not sure that I do. Time for what? To chill, he says. At that moment I check my phone and see that a girl has posted a selfie to Facebook with the caption:

> Spring is here, I look like I'm dying lol

Reduced to the negligible poverty of remaining earth available to her, a little frame on a cell phone she's died within for the cuteness of the world has been vastly damaged, gasp or whatever. I'll take of it what I can, get high, ask Anton what he means by time. 'I don't think we have time,' he clarifies, 'or not in a way that isn't fought for.' Therefore implicit is the injunction to seek new, still more tenuous martyrdoms via the terms of employment, daily baptism through which we are made eternal pilgrims to global capital's realm of internationalised leisure, various martyrdoms we will survive without the redemptive pleasure of extended vacation. Or rather, it grants us in the flavorless wafer of its inexorable host our own host body by which we hobble forward until the endurable progress of this narrative reverses and we are erased from it. The city lights go on. The view has become the same everywhere. You can tell it won't change.

This boy I follow on Instagram photographed himself in a bathtub full of little slices of cucumbers, some of which he placed under his soaked white T-shirt like strange nipples. There's something almost puritanical in how the white tub, white T-shirt, and green vegetables have been linked together on my narrow iPhone screen in spare form, charged by some singular force that arrives in reverence for transcendence of flesh via the various systems of information exchange that carry his image to me. According to the geotag feature on Instagram, he's based in South East London, somewhere near Goldsmiths, though only one photograph indicates where he was when he took it, so he could be anywhere for that matter. He could still be in the tub, adrift in the lazy mist of cucumber water, hand poised overhead to selfie the moment into the cloud. When I show his picture to Kevin, Kevin says, 'I think he's a J. W. Anderson model.' 'Definitely not,' I say. I keep tagging Kevin in his photos to see if we can get his attention, but nothing comes of it. Like, flirtations without the real, there's nothing to be had except some dumb semblance of sex in the heady air of my feed, whatever that might mean. I do actually get kind of hard at the thought of him in London looking at Instagram and wondering who I might be, in New York, tagging someone named Kevin, also in New York. Or hardness isn't the word so much as it's a dowsing sense of a person who couldn't care less and as such lingers at the magnetic zero-point of some entropic bliss that places me in front of the mirror, thinking about him and checking myself out to see why my body isn't as nice as his. We are not the same. I put on a white shirt and get into the tub with my phone. Everything must eventually get out of hand.

It is easy to say nothing. Nearly every song I've ever heard says nothing, whether by accident or intention. In Welcome to New York, which often plays on the radio, Taylor Swift greets a terrifying nowhere that supposes inclusion while ensuring the door to the city is locked. Rihanna's We Found Love is the opposite, but to describe either or do the work that insists that these particular evocations of sudden solidarity with others matters now or will in a future that most certainly will never come seems a little flawed. Like can't you stop, because the cessation of these interests that supposedly transcend my life for the Top 40 or the iTunes Top 10 is totally dumb. I suppose I can but isn't Taylor's best friend Lorde cute when she hunches up Gollum-like to paw at the camera? I've always identified with this position: the sixteen-year-old who, unsure of how to act at the Grammys, only acts, flailing and throwing herself about, liberated of those constraints of taste that might restrain her from behaving a little dorky on stage. I suppose the intersection of these desires presents a challenge I would like to refuse. I find myself believing that my language is failing me while it succeeds for everyone else. Flailing about, my vocabulary gets lost in loopy grammar yet I suspect the generally implied super-connection of language is still achievable if I continue to work at it. But the assumption that, no matter what, you can say *something* remains awfully common, regardless of evidence to the contrary. Grievances of this kind should not accumulate. On Twitter, Jackie Wang has been quoting Hélène Cixous, someone I'm embarrassed to admit I've never read. Wang quotes:

> 'Because she arrives, vibrant, over and again, we are at the beginning of a new history.'

Wang tweets that Cixous didn't begin to write until she was twenty seven and:

> I'm trying to remind myself that this is only the beginning.

I am, too. She continues to quote Cixous:

> 'I am spacious, singing flesh, on which is grated no one knows which I, more or less human, but alive because of transformation.'

One minute later:

> 'Her libido is cosmic, just as her unconscious is worldwide. Her writing can only keep going.'

One minute later:

> 'she goes and passes into infinity.'

The same minute:

> 'She alone dares and wishes to know from within, where she, the outcast, has never ceased to hear the resonance of fore-language.'

Two minutes later:

> 'airborne swimmer, in flight, she does not cling to herself; she is dispersible, prodigious, stunning, desirous & capable of others.'

With this I am reminded, somewhat simultaneously, of two unrelated things: (1) Kathy Acker's line from *Demonology, My Mother*: 'Red was the colour of wildness and of what is as yet unknown,' red being many things for Acker, including nightmare, passion, journeys into the interior, hidden flesh, the unconscious, rage, and violence; and (2) Jackie Wang's *Against Innocence*, her refutation of the liberal politics of 'innocence' and their direct appeal to the white imaginary, which upholds the dominant social structures which declare the bodies of others criminal in order to 'cleanse' urban spaces for whites. Of course there's a lot more – and the impulse to summarise is itself a kind of violence – but she's continued to tweet Cixous and I returned to my feed:

> 'In one another we will never be lacking.'

A minute later:

> 'Each body distributes in its own special way, without model or norm, the nonfinite and changing totality of its desires.'

And finally:

> 'we're not going to repress something so simple as the desire for life.'

This afternoon I walked home in the snow from my boyfriend's and felt a fussy sadness that left me a sludge of indistinct feelings. The night before we had stayed up till 3:00 AM waiting for a 'potentially historic Nor'easter' that never came, though what of the blizzard did come to New York City dropped a considerable amount of snow on the ground. Walking I thought that maybe there was a poem I'd read at some point about unrealised blizzards but I couldn't remember who wrote it or if it even existed. Poetry is an idiotic impulse but it is exactly this quality that makes it worthwhile, linked to idiocy by way of the history of that word, which comes from the Greek and means private person. Poetry is a form of privacy and as everyone knows privacy is idiotic. Again, grievances of this kind should not accumulate.

Desire is Irrelevant. or Is It?

Omar Kholeif

The water doesn't make me nauseous anymore, but I need to pee. Lap-lap-lap, back and forth, thrif-thrif-thrif, gruf, gruf, gruf, the grinding of a waterbus engine.

Don't explode!

A kid's soccer team gets onto the boat, the bus. They fill the whole thing. Like ants, they take over and enrapture. The pungent smell of sweaty scrotums tickles my nose; it bristles.

A beautiful round arse bludgeons my face. By accident?

I am standing anchored on the interior nozzle of the boat. Half inside, half out.

The sumptuous bottom is warmed and encased by a pair

of combat trousers (cargo pants).

So 1990s, post-grunge era. So not even Eurotrash. So mid-1940s USA. So not interested. I came to Venice for a Rudolph Valentino.

He turns around and smiles, 'Okay, perhaps I was wrong,' I ponder – that is, until he drops his giant bag onto my foot. I scream. Inside, of course. Outside I am ultra-masc, post-metrosexual. Post-sexual, even. Emotion: Zero.

CUT TO

Ferocious clouds are engulfing the Sunday sky.

I am waiting for a friend. An artist. The son of Venetian aristocracy.

He transpires. He is standing before a silver lion that is mounted on a plinth near San Marco Square.

The artist traipses towards me, his gazelle-like figure cutting through the winter chill.

His body begins to fill my vision. The people in the square start to diminish. My body turns to ice as he inches closer. My heart starts to pump faster. I hurl forward to touch him. I'm nervous that he might turn into stone.

I am in a glass case of my own making. The Evil Eye is holding me hostage. The world will stop unless I unbuckle its grip. I remember the prayers my mother used to say to ward off the demons. I recite one of them in my head.

The church bell is sounding.

The artist takes my hand and we skip forward like two models in the pages of a *W Magazine* photo shoot. We've been cast with no specific instruction but to be happy and to produce a dream-like image for those around, watching us.

Five, maybe ten minutes pass. He stops and gazes at me.

He wants me to meet his new lover.

'My wounded Cupid,' he calls him.

A young man with protruding fish-like eyes reaches out to shake my hand. His wispy hair pokes out from under his beanie cap. He has a *Heartbreak High* kind of aesthetic.

'Gio is an opera singer!'

The young man grimaces, turns around and starts to limp forward. He points out a small golden door – a back passage into the church.

His hand dangles backwards and grabs the artist's hand affectionately. All of a sudden I feel lonelier than I have ever felt, possibly in my entire life. Like I am entering into the sacred passage of God's hotel room, only God's angel doesn't want me in there. I have somehow forced my way into heaven to see if it's for real, only to realise that my sins will forever outweigh any good deeds that would allow me to taste its fruit.

A tear falls from my lazy eye and burns my skin. I awkwardly follow Gio through the back door.

The beauty inside is unbearable. This is a cathedral. Byzantine-style gold icons hover over and swallow all that is beneath.

Gio makes like a good choirboy and departs for his position.

We are in Sunday mess. The priest begins to speak.

A boy begins to sing, only to quickly be interrupted by the priest again.

I turn to my neighbour. 'Is this what it's always like?'

The man in front of me turns around and shooshes me, his spiky finger placed perfectly over his lip.

'Fascist,' says the artist. I smirk.

I peer at the fascist's back and I am mesmerised by the length of his shoulders. This man, eighty years old now, must have been a swimmer once upon a time, maybe an Olympic swimmer, who spent his life only ever reaching for Bronze.

A pregnant lady with the most beautiful face suddenly moves in next to me along the pew. I adore pregnant women. They must all be good people. I am sure of it. Only horrible people like me would want to live a life alone in isolation. Surely moms or mums as they are called are all filled with lavish love, even if their greedy appetites might suggest otherwise.

The cue to sit:

> Brothers and sisters, this is what I mean: our time is growing short. Those who have wives should live as though they had none, and those who mourn should live as though they had nothing to mourn for; those who are enjoying life should live as though there were nothing to laugh about; those whose life is buying things should live as though they had nothing of their own; and those who have to deal with the world should not become engrossed in it.

'How To Not Be Engrossed.' I shall write the guidebook.

A young man materialises on stage. It is not Gio. Gio is in the background, not to be seen today. I am relieved. I never want to see him again.

He starts to sing. I could swear he is a Castrato – a boy. His balls chopped off by his mother to preserve his voice. He waves his left hand. At first, his gesture seems effervescent. He continues to sing – buzzing, purring, and intoning.

If this were a musical I would lunge forward through the air and lift the boy up by his waist. We would float together in circular gestures, whooshing through the dome of the cathedral. I would beg everyone to leave, so that it could be him and me alone, for eternity. We would drip with emotion; I would devour him and let him devour me. We would unfold the archaeology of each other's imagination until there was nothing left concealed.

I am leaving this island to go back to mine: a constellation of islands in the Mediterranean Sea.

But before I know it, the captain of my ship has made a U-turn.

There is more work to be done on this island before I can leave, he informs me.

Tiny Struggles

Lynne Tillman

He managed the walk to Main Street, three blocks, two long avenues, and didn't worry about how he looked – a big whitehead poking along the sidewalk. Things were getting better, not that Tiny knew the absolute right moment to leave his house, because out the back door his garden merged with theirs, and the neighbors might be around. Summer weekends, everyone hung out.

He could leave through the front door, but that resembled a first entrance in the middle of the second act, which was why, finally, Tiny quit acting. That excruciating second, when his presence on stage was unmistakably felt, disarmed him nightly. Even appearing in the soaps got to him, but he'd made a bundle. Tiny's new existence in the country was awkward, remarkable – remarked upon by those who knew him – exciting, and maybe permanent. He'd figure it out as he went along.

'It's not really the country, the row houses on your block, they're city structures,' one friend said.

'You're in the hood,' another said. 'The ghetto.'

'It's a mixed nabe,' Tiny said, imitating a nightly news guy, the face of the real America.

Not much separated the houses, a few feet, low fences, honeysuckle, ugly weed trees no one bothered to dig up. To build high fences or plant overbearing trees could appear unneighborly or sinister. Inside his private domain, anything was possible, he could do anything, but he didn't, no one does, or few do, anyway. No one used all his freedom, and, wherever Tiny was, nameless others entered his mental space.

Upon waking, Tiny pulled the curtains half-open, for some natural light and to show the neighbors he had nothing to hide. To his left, the neighbors were also city converts, professional people, architect and designer, a black and white couple, Nicholas and Arthur, who kept to themselves and had friends over occasionally. Tiny was invited when he first arrived, but informally they agreed to preserve a sense of the city and be neighbors who borrow a figurative cup of sugar.

Most days and nights, the street was dead quiet. A few shouts and bursts of loud music, nothing much. The other night, or early morning, was anomalous, because Tiny woke up to cries and yowls that wolves make when their cubs are killed or kidnapped. An obese white woman, who sat on her ruined porch every warm day and night, was wailing to a disheveled, skinny man, 'You're not leaving are you … ? You're not leaving me are you … ? You're not walking out are you … ? You're not you can't leave me … !' Tiny squirmed below the window ledge. No one had ever yowled at him, he found it kind of magnificent – the passion. Nothing like that, unless he counted the stinging email rebukes from his older sister, Georgina.

> Tiny, On the phone, you acted like everything was fine and dandy between us, and I'm supposed to pretend the way you do. You feel your behavior doesn't call for an apology. But when your friend's dog bit me on the calf, and their dog went RIGHT FOR ME, instead of comforting me, you said the bite was nothing, Look, you're not bleeding, you said. Nothing, no compassion. How would you like it if ...

Family. Tiny couldn't escape them, even now, three hours away from them and their city. He was the baby and the tallest, perversely nicknamed Tiny. His given name was Theodore, after the fat Roosevelt, which his father thought was funny. His father had bought the farm six years ago, his mother was doing the big fade, and before he moved away, Tiny had split with his girlfriend of six years. His twin brothers were jerks, and his sister was angry at him for being born.

It was a new life he wanted.

Some stores in town were easier to enter than others. Some owners or managers welcomed him, some greasily, others held back, restraint or contempt, he couldn't judge. He was no judge, that was his father. This afternoon, the pale, lithe woman in the cheese store, her blond hair screwed into a furious top knot, seemed disagreeable. Tiny intuited that Top Knot despised selling jams and cage-free eggs from happy chickens. This is where I end up, she's thinking, slicing a chunk of aged Gouda for ... She couldn't find words for him, Tiny decided – what and who was this tall, forty-something, pale-skinned, dark-haired man in faded jeans and an unironed shirt, untucked. He watched her, fascinated.

It was an up-and-coming town, at least it had been up-and-coming when he bought the house; now people were saying it would come back. The town will come back, you'll see, it always comes back. The town thrived and failed, an organism dependent on visitors who savored its Victorian houses and country-style stores selling thick bars of French soap and 1920s dish towels laundered in bleach. Now Tiny was moving through a fastidious space. He picked up a bath-sized fluffy white towel, which could wrap a small car, and fingered its thick pile. He hovered over an ample bunch of dried lavender, whose scent offered instant sanity.

Mostly, the native population was out of work, blacks, whites, integrated and equally downhearted. The town-kids' future didn't seem unknowable: taxes low, public schools abysmal. More and more stray cats, who would never be neutered, screamed in Tiny's garden, because he liked cats and fed them scraps when no one was around. His sister always said, 'You make your own messes.' He couldn't walk on the grass without sliding in shit.

Main Street stretched on and on against real time. Tiny strolled toward an unhurried café or good bar; he wasn't hunting, exactly. The best bar in town served a mixed-up-everything clientele, and weekend nights drew a big crowd from surrounding towns smaller than his. His town. Our town. Above the bar's spotted mirror, to the left, Tiny read reassuring words on an old-fashioned black board.

> *Use PARA-word in sentence. Your sentence wins – Martini on the house!*
>
> *That Victorian she couldn't afford – paradise.*
>
> *He advertised in the local paper for a paramour. His bad!*

Tiny usually needed an incentive and took a seat at the long, white marble-topped bar. The only person he'd ever met, down one end, was a solitary, bookish man who dressed up as James Joyce, so Tiny forgot his name because he unfailingly thought: James Joyce.

> *Paradox, paralysis, parasite, parataxis, parallel.*

Near Mr Joyce, ignoring him, an exasperated fifty-ish man exclaimed to his group, 'It's not the fine arts, it's the construction business.' Down the other end of the long bar, a svelte woman about his age peered at him. He drank his vodka tonic. She peered again. Tiny smiled. She peered again, anxiously. He walked over to be friendly.

'Do we know each other?' Tiny said.

'I'm sorry, I thought you were someone else. I'm not wearing my glasses.'

'But I am someone else.' Tiny said.

She looked perplexed, not amused, so he tipped his

invisible hat and returned to his end of the bar.

Paradoxically, the fox …

He finished another vodka, another sentence.

Who doesn't long to be a parasite and never work?

He handed the paper to the red-faced, buxom bartender. 'No good deed goes unpunished, no bad deed goes unpublished,' he murmured intimately, to restore his cool. This is a wit's end, he told himself.

Life's just full of niggling compromise. Tiny wouldn't sweat the small things, that was city life. Walking home along the dreamy back alley, Tiny fed his fantasies, starting one, re-playing it, she's on her knees, starting another, staring at the huge, blue sky, sun still a flaming red ball. The new version fails to start, he can't get it started, but how can he fail at his own fantasy. Defeated, momentarily, Tiny remembered his college friend Tom, who looked upset one morning in the cafeteria. Tom habitually dreamed he was flying.

'Last night,' Tom said, 'I couldn't get lift-off.'

His neighbors Nick and Arthur's lights were on, three more cars in their parking area meant guests, while his other next-door neighbors – renters not owners – sat at a long, wooden picnic table, eating corn and hot dogs. Barbecue smells, country life, the sweet life.

'Nice evening, folks, how're you doing?'

'Just great, how're you doing?' one of the men said.

Five adults and one child lived upstairs in the two-story house: two stringy white guys, one hefty black woman, one scrawny white one, all in their thirties; a lean, light-skinned black woman, twenty maybe, and a ten year old white boy. Tiny had heard the boy call both men 'Daddy'. He couldn't tell them apart, either. The family must view him as a weirdo. The weirdo in their midst. The scrawny, white woman took her time responding, as if on delay. 'We're fine, thank you … and how are you?' She had a singsong voice, and emphasised 'and how'. He dubbed her the ironic one. The lean, young woman appeared to be sulking, her thin face drawn with cheekbones like flying buttresses. She didn't greet him at all, she scarcely raised her head, but he wished she had. Her name was Chelsea, her black cat, Satan. Unfixed, he was sure.

The old sun started its descent, and Tiny was aloft on his terrace, squinting at the newspaper, and watching the birds on his lawn – sparrows – peck away at masses of birdseed he'd thrown into a super-large metal salad bowl. The birdseed company advertised its seed as irresistible to colourful birds – he'd had two blue jays, one redbreasted robin. Hundreds of sparrows arrived the same time every morning and evening, positioned on the electric wires, a scene from *The Birds*, until he refilled the bowl. No one else fed the birds the way he did.

This was great, this was better than living in the country, he reckoned – it was sort of a city in the country, with benefits like gardening, feeding birds and stray cats, renewal along with the seasons, the chance to be natural and free, because things were different here.

Tiny fixed himself another vodka. Everyone spied

on their neighbors, and why he cared about getting caught or being nosy, he didn't know, except it conformed with his being citified, a veneer to shed. Tonight, a large white-frosted cake appeared, ablaze with candles – the birthday of the scrawny woman, thirty five. The neighbors to their right, who kept a beautiful garden, were barbecuing in tandem; by outward appearances, they were white, one father, one mother, two sons, the traditional family. The hulking blond boys, close in age, nineteen or twenty, stood at the fence flirting with Chelsea. She leaned in, they leaned in, three bodies pressed against the flimsy barrier. He wondered which one she would choose. Not him, that was certain.

Tiny followed the progress of Chelsea's romance like a sitcom, a week of day-time backyard flirting and fence-leaning, the brothers in baggy shorts, she in her polka dot bikini, then night-time hanging out, until one evening Tiny spotted Chelsea in the other backyard, at their dinner table, while her family, eating their dinner, glanced at that other backyard, ruefully, and he thought, like a soothsayer, there's going to be trouble.

It didn't take long, Chelsea selected the bigger of the two. Tiny tried to gainsay why, because they both appeared to be good-natured hunks. Maybe one had a great personality or was a better kisser. Chelsea and the boyfriend pitched a tent for two in his family's backyard, and every night, they'd disappear, and every morning, she'd scoot back to her house, or, if she'd gone home to sleep, Tiny would awaken to the boy's calling her name, sort of mournfully, 'Chel-seeeee,' She'd emerge from her house, sleep-deprived and sleepy-faced, and glowing. 'Chel-seeeee ...' Chelsea began saying Hello to him, too. And then the boys did. She was blooming in her new world, from the looks of it a better one.

The two families didn't actually acknowledge each other. They weren't feuding but there was a gulf between them. Like families separated by the Berlin Wall, some in the East, some the West, unable to communicate, raised so differently. Satan regularly jumped over the fence into the wrong yard, and Chelsea carried him back, not saying a word, returning quickly to the other side. More and more, the scrawny woman turned her back to the girl, who was or wasn't her daughter, as Chelsea raced to that other backyard. And the scrawny woman started leaving garbage near Tiny's side of the fence, not taking it to the dump. When it started to stink real bad, he'd talk to her, gently.

The August weather lay heavily on everyone, oppressive as the country's news. Tiny couldn't eat dinner in front of the TV anymore, not at news time; and he couldn't avoid any of it, not by turning on the A/C or the TV. Things seeped in. Tiny and his one-way street were at peace, nothing grievous happening, the obese woman sat on her ruined porch like a Buddha, the skinny man coming and going, kids played in the street, and the guys next door became friendlier, by attrition if nothing else.

In October, the weather changed to bright and zesty, plants dying, trees bursting with Fall. Tiny's days were okay, a little boring, or too good, so he knew it would change, because everything changed – better or worse, there was always change. 'You can count on that,' his mother used to say, before her dementia set in. Tiny would need to find work soon, but maybe he wouldn't be able to. He might fall in love, even with Top Knot. He might win the lottery, but if he won millions, so much he didn't know what to do with it, that would become a burden. Most lottery winners led rotten lives ever after, hounded by relatives, and some killed themselves. He would apologise to his sister, and promise her money when she needed it.

The weather turned colder, his first winter in the country.

He bundled into his old, heavy coat, swung his gray wool scarf around his neck, found a tote bag, and opened his front door to the world. He'd walk to Main Street, do his shopping, visit Top Knot, who had her moments. He didn't get far. Chelsea was standing in front of her house, her belongings on the street. Everything, all her clothes and CDs, had been flung out from the second floor. Five big, shapeless mounds. Chelsea, in only a T-shirt and jeans, was gathering up what she could, putting it in black garbage bags, and crying without making a sound. Tiny gathered stuff too and set it on the sidewalk. They did that together, silently, until her boyfriend showed up. He embraced Chelsea and looked at Tiny.

'They kicked her out,' the boyfriend said.

'Kicked her out,' Tiny said.

'Yeah, the shits kicked her out.'

'Why? What happened?'

'Because she doesn't have a job. None of them got a job, but they kick her out, and she's just eighteen.'

'She's jealous,' Chelsea said. 'She's jealous of me.'

Tiny knew she was the scrawny blond.

'Chelsea's got nowhere to go,' the boyfriend said.

'Nowhere to go,' Tiny said.

The words sounded like stones.

The three stood together, Chelsea bending in toward her boyfriend for protection against the wind. They looked at him intently.

They wanted him to offer her a place to stay for a while, he had a house all to himself. He couldn't. It would turn bad. He just couldn't.

'Jesus,' Tiny said, 'this is really terrible.'

'I don't know what I'm going to do,' Chelsea said.

'She can't stay with us, me and my brother and her, and my parents,' the boyfriend said. 'It can't happen.'

The wind whipped around them, and Tiny drew his scarf up near his mouth. He could pretend to be tone deaf or blind. He could explain that his mother was coming to live with him. But then it might happen. Stranger things than that happen.

'I'm sorry. I'm really sorry. I wish I could help you. You'll find someplace.'

'Yeah,' the boyfriend said, 'social services or something.'

'Something's gotta happen,' Chelsea said.

'It always does. Something happens. You can count on things to change,' Tiny said.

He could see their hope collapse. The three of them stood there, then the two of them looked at each other, maybe for strength, Tiny thought later. Chelsea faced him, purposefully.

'You one of those toxic bachelors,' she said.

'Me? What do you mean?'

'You know, a fickle dude. A love 'em and leave 'em guy,' she said.

'I'm not …'

'You know, ambiguous,' she said.

Ambivalent, she means, but he wasn't going there.

'I just like living alone, that's all.'

'Everyone has to live with themselves,' the boyfriend said.

'Yeah,' Chelsea said, 'you have to live with yourself.'

She said it fiercely. Tiny could protest more that he wasn't toxic, but it might be better to let her think he was ambiguous. 'Toxic bachelor' must be a reality show. He pulled his scarf tighter. It was freezing. She must be freezing, he thought. But she held her head higher.

'I can take care of your cat,' he said.

It was a gesture.

'Satan?' Chelsea said.

'Sure, I can do that, if you want. I can take care of him for a while. If you want.'

Chelsea studied him, her boyfriend studied him. They glanced at each other. It took a stupefyingly long time, and the ball was in her court. It was her call.

'No way, no fucking way,' Chelsea said, fiercer now. 'My cat goes with me.'

She and her boyfriend bent down, grabbed some clothes, and carried the stuff toward the alley.

The way Tiny told it to close friends, he'd given her room so she could reject him. He wouldn't ever know what she thought. Chelsea moved the next day. The scrawny woman's garbage stayed there, along with Chelsea's clothes, frozen, for a long time. Tiny heard rumors about where Chelsea lived and with whom, but the boyfriend didn't follow after her. That surprised him.

Animals of Rotterdam Zoo

CHRIS MCCORMACK

Flamingos reflected in water. One bird's head at the leg of another. Their beaks separating the mud from the brine shrimp. An amount of birds on a tree branch. Identifying some animals was difficult due to the Dutch-only signage. I can only say that they are birds, all sitting quietly.

I had stripped and showered before I turned on the slide-projector. Changing clothes in the middle of the day seems like a simple stepping between various recollections of sex. I had done that thing again of wearing only my boxers all day, playing with my nipple hair, and waiting for my dead-sea face mask to dry an ash solid.

A large egret, next to shards of bamboo. In the background of the same photograph, two women are visible; one wears a crimson shirt, coming into focus. The other blends into the background, a sort of camouflage of blonde hair and smoke.

I am watching a slideshow of animals taken in Rotterdam Zoo at my flat in London. I've set the slides to change every twenty seconds, or thereabouts. I took all the photographs recently while having heart palpitations; a condition brought about by swallowing five white diet pills with two shots of Jack Daniels and a beer in a sunburst cut glass. An attractive friend, who I had met briefly once before, confidently suggest that we take them. On his gay-tourists map, he had listed various sex-shops on streets he called 'shame-straats'. He had an ability to make everything seem singularly and instantaneously desirable. Or was it just him, and his off-register eyebrows as we browsed fisting DVDs in homemade packaging? As a note, the label on the diet pills read: two to four in 24 hours, without alcohol. The palpitations, although less common or extreme, are still continuing. I try to keep the photographs in the order that I had encountered the animals.

A bird-watching shed, no birds. Momentary desolation. Pinned to the dampened wood slatted walls is a newly printed poster indicating various animal species. Two terrapins clamped together in stone-felt sex; another appears to be watching with its mouth stretched open like an out-turned pocket.

Feeling close to black out, blood-pushed collapse, or close to something not my understanding, I sat at a table, listening to a live band play Misty or Misty Blue or Blue Moon or variations of notes and noise. I re-read the pills' ingredients as a way to try and undo the content's effects, folding and refolding the branded napkins and out-of-bound enzymes between my fingers and thoughts with restricted distraction. I relinquish the bottle of pills as a gift to a woman who orders water for me, twice, with words. She was amused by the drawing of the sprinting woman on the bottle. With the bottle and ingredient list now gone, the link to the process that was happening inside loosens. Watching the waiters turn the chairs upside down with tired and determined intent, I allow myself to drop from consciousness. My feet heavy with heat and blood.

I put on clean black socks, and notice how a simple completeness is achieved with socks on. Brown animals missing sections of hair. It gives them a wild, mistreated look that is uncertain to a visitor worrying about zoo ethics such as myself. Perhaps this hair loss happens anyway. Traces of saliva are visible in the sunlight. Their bodies contain moisture in large volumes that in my head break up like dots of earth.

I stayed at a friend's rented flat that night. It confirmed that he really did wear black underwear. He found white too expected, clinical, post-image. I watch him sleep. I sit like a transfixed cat at a tomb of my own making watching the sun come up, counting each minute into each hour. The skylight turning from dark portal to light source. My constant unnerving awareness of his rises and falls of consciousness through the night. I sat upright looking at a collection of drying potted plants. Words cannot be printed fast enough for these kinds of things.

Two buffalos sit in bright sunlight; one grazes a patch of grass. I noticed that this morning my gums and orifices bled more readily than usual. I swallow this casually of inner destruction. My body: a temple collapsing in a bull ring of self-absorption. The paycheck of all these physical tremors and body temperature changes arrives to only make this further deficit of understanding: I am staggeringly awake. Small rodent-like creatures; a man is visible in the background, his large telephoto lens covering his face like a terrorist's balaclava. Their pinkish eyes shot out with Canon flash in the dark. Children's fingerprints caught on the edge of the glass, each mark looks to have tried to count each rat.

Lying on the restrictively-sized hotel bed later the next day, I feel my body move remotely above the cotton as it slips over the plastic undersheet. I watch an antiques programme on a wall-bracketed television near ceiling height. I drink water. I should have bought still water, not sparkling. I was feeling killed by partially excited water. I contemplate how long it might take before it gets flat and wonder if I might be dead by then. The sound of heavy drilling into soft concrete starts from somewhere upstairs, this being lawfully permitted daytime noise. I turn the television volume up and hear the antique auctioneer complete bids. The drilling then stops, and all the rumples in the bed become noticeable in the passing sunlight.

Small frogs pressed against glass, tiled with condensation bubbles. Black eyes motionless, their soft, egg yolk density green bodies baking out under my clumsy watch. I start regulating my breathing with Scuba-like instruction to the slide-projector's rhythmic shuffling of slides. The climb and fall of biology and reaction under light.

At Rotterdam's Accident and Emergency I speak blankly to the hospital receptionist that I had neither the money nor the health insurance. I wasn't really sure if I had either, or if I had a reason genuine enough to be admitted, but in any case, I was. I was given an ECG, a 'map of the heart' the doctor said, as if knowing only half its meaning. It almost moved me to tears. I had forgotten that some of my organs had existed. She took a blood sample. Instead of a regular plaster on my arm, the doctor placed a hard round sponge more commonly used in dentistry. Helps prevent bruising she said, framing all these needs with the empty precision of a hospital bed corner. Her material wisdom felt part of a different order that I could only ever glimpse at during these heightened moments of potential death.

The tropical house. The bright sadness of a toucan looking up from behind, its orange beak partly visible. Its waxy tail flanked with white. I imagine reaching and touching it, all hard beak and half-alive body stiffening from touch, and it wanting to hurt me in response. I began to wonder which are the most photographed animals and if there is a study of animal favouritism in public places that lead to selection processes quite beyond the comprehension of most visitors. I closed my eyes and pictured sleeping toucans.

The doctor left the curtain open and as people walked past I felt a sense of belonging. I was now a tableau of natural and unquestionable concern. I had given my body over to a history of finely-tuned physical obsession. A throne to watch life pass by with a tube taped into my mouth. I devote each calibrated breath to be the same as the last in length and strength, to try and screw myself back to a god-needed normalcy. It was the kind of place that you want your friends to visit, as if the hospital was built for you. The reverie of passing through corridors of clean thermoset plastic, navigated by one's singular diagnostic needs in a language that can never be understood, just relievedly trusted upon. I was discharged after a couple of hours with the temporary desire to send the nurses the most exaggeratedly colourful flowers I could. Any underlying sense of misappropriated medical attention was suppressed as I passed a row of policemen at the exit.

Field mice buried in what looks like shredded statistic papers. Only one head is visible. I notice the simulation of day and night areas for the little animals and feel caught in the twilight of cold observation. I think back to watching my boyfriend sleep the other night, thinking how I feel so far from that, how far the drop-frame rate of our relationship has increased to a point that leaves only static and dull witnessing of time's passing. Darwin once wrote that the suffering of the lower animals throughout time was more than he could bear to think of. Increasingly, my compassion starts to feel like a lost symbol on the periodic table. Each slide mechanically pulled out and dropped from view.

A grey seal, silt covers the viewing glass. I stop, turn off the radio, and look out of my window and see five teenagers eating Halal meat on bicycles; they all look up at me. In my mind this kind of event has possible repercussions, such as small stones or coins being thrown at your window when you turn the lights out at night. I close the curtains and hear my boyfriend come home. In the distance a woman in a bright red jacket feeds several penguins small fish.

I look at the empty bed. I look at it, and how the way I've slept in it has changed the original colour of the fabric over time, how I keep waking up at night having heart palpitations; waiting for my breath to fix itself or me back into unconsciousness. And the soft memory of the shape of a stranger's armpit over my face as we practiced convincingly unsafe sex a few weeks ago. All of life rolled-up under that body part of his. I hold onto that and stare at my pillows. My heart rate climbs again with the tensile tightness of reptilian control.

In the taxi to Rotterdam's A&E I made a phone call to my brother. I was laughing, to the surprise of the driver. He asked me if I was the patient, I smiled and said yes. I knew I wasn't a very believable ill person, but then I also wanted to distance myself from what was happening. I then attempted to revise the story to the driver, effectively rewriting it to fit his version of the reality that I was scrambling inside of. I repeated that he must have misheard me, that I was, in all truth, visiting someone. As a result I was driven to a different end of the car park. I walked across several lanes of traffic to the entrance I needed, wondering if I could have a Dutch friend that I might be visiting, what their name might be if so. Honking his horn, the taxi driver shouted I was going the wrong direction, I had to pretend I didn't hear him.

A seahorse, in classical profile. The kind of photograph that really didn't require you to take it because it already exists. I am semi-relieved that it may in fact be from another person's photographic slideshow.

I stop and listen to my boyfriend on the phone. He is running his hand under the elastic of his sock while staring into space. I think of doing something similar to occupy the time, but wait instead. I notice I am semi-erect. He sits next to me. 'You're busy,' he says to someone on the phone. He comes off the phone, only to say he wants to sleep. I feel slightly short changed. I slip my hand under my underwear and feel around for something and find only skin. When I was a teenager, I would measure the quantity of sperm after masturbating. A plastic cup that was intended to measure the quantities of cough syrup for children and adults, now carefully adopted for my newfound pleasures. The average male ejaculation learnt in science class compared and contrasted against my own efforts behind closed doors. The basic knowledge that hydration improves ejaculatory amounts. I used to keep the cup under my bed, I cannot remember ever washing it out.

Undeterminable animal in water, its pale body moving through strands of sandpaper grey weeds. Frogspawn. The bathroom ventilation system that continues for longer than seemingly necessary extensions of time; a moisturiser with its lid off and collecting dust for days on end. Scooped out like avocado and accidentally dropping to the floor.

I lean back in my chair and feel the pressed, fine cotton shirt rise out of my trousers and the small draft on exposed skin. I watch my boyfriend comb his hair, brush his teeth. I watch him. He sleeps. I think about the speed of my heart rate, I concentrate on whether it is normal, or raised. Speeding up, or slowing. I no longer can tell, my insides feel as vague as a zig-zag patterned shower curtain.

The coastal section of the zoo display. Bones and cold water, the dull stink of sulphur. A sea anemone perched on a recreation of a coral reef; the trace of a gunpowder substance darkening its edges. Sponges and minor fish are indicated in the gloom, not unlike the memory of watching a woman's plastic bag split open on the bus and her tangerines rolling down the aisle, flashing brightly against the grey.

I open an online chat room to an East European man who likes groups. He describes himself. I describe myself. I'm not this person, but then I suspect he is not the person that he is describing either. I type about the last time I got fucked. I remember the tilting back of my head, which I describe as being:

Forced and gagged ...

The pulling of each other's Adidas shorts down, which I describe as:

Ripped off ...

An image of gazelle standing motionless. He hadn't ejaculated inside me, although I said he did. I'd almost like to think he did. But then I wouldn't have been able to measure the amount, like I did. I stop typing, close the laptop and think about how his fart had filled the room with a burning wood smell. I amuse myself with possibilities of cedar versus spruce. The deduction of difference being turned back to indeterminate vegetation like a child's felt tip drawing.

Sheep in a field with an upturned blue barrel. Then a photo of me taken by a Dutch woman. I'm standing by the prairie dogs, my expression is happy, I think, or maybe I'm hesitatingly caught not knowing if she has yet pressed the shutter release.

Flamboyant Rose

Jessey Tsang

Guangzhou station, crowded and wet, is a notoriously difficult place for hailing cabs. The driver looked at my muddy legs with disgust. Ignoring his stare, I hopped onto the taxi with my newly bought, also muddy red high-heels. I took off my shoes in the taxi. 'Please driver,' I said with my limited Mandarin, 'take me to Tianhe, Linhe Middle Road, The Deluse.' Staring out at the misty, nameless roads, I wondered why I was there, after telling myself I wouldn't go. I'd even pushed the meeting I had on the next day to the next week, ignoring glances from my colleagues, and left with my new red shoes on. The driver drove around Tianhe many times but could not find the restaurant. I think he was from another district, that or the restaurant wasn't in fact very famous. Finally, he found it. I paid and rushed out.

There was a huge sign saying 'Cheung and Wang's

wedding' outside the restaurant. I hoped I wasn't too late. It was 7:00 PM, around the time wedding banquets started in Hong Kong. I had heard that Northern people had their weddings in the mornings, and weddings in the afternoon were usually for second marriages. Two people who were not from Guangzhou having their wedding in Guangzhou was a real test for their friends and relatives. I wondered who the wild Ka Sai finally settled down with. What kind of person was he, and how did he manage to convince Ka Sai to marry him and move back to mainland?

'Chan Mei Ling! Chan Mei Ling!' A girl with long, curly hair ran towards me from the stairs and threw her arms around me. 'I knew you'd come!' she said excitedly. 'I knew you'd come, I've missed you! Ka Sai would be so happy to know you're here!' Some time ago I picked up the talent for being calm. I smiled, 'We actually never hung out much in the past, call me Ling! It's been a while since I've been called my full name.' Cooled down by my coldness, she took me into the banquet hall.

The doors opened and I was blinded by flashes. Everyone surrounded the newlyweds' table. After taking my gift, the reception asked me if I was friends with the bride or the groom. I never understood the point of this question. If it was just to differentiate the gifts, why not just split them evenly? I answered the question in my mind: I fell out with the bride and have no interest in being friends with the groom. I left the reception and walked toward the crowd. The hall was filled with red roses and CoCo Chanel N°5 fragrance. Ka Sai had always loved this scent. Our school garden was full of red roses. Once, Ka Sai pricked herself on a rose and fell in love with roses ever since. I said roses were outdated and I only liked lilies. I didn't look at roses with her, but I did take her to my mum's room to secretly use her Chanel N°5 fragrance. Ka Sai said she only liked this fragrance. All the fragrances that boys had bought her through the years,

Dior

Gucci

Kenzo ...

They all ended up in my room.

When I approached the crowd, there were cheers all around. Oh God, I thought, don't tell me it was time for the bouquet throwing. And please don't let it land in my hands. 'Girls, get ready! Who wants to be lucky like me?' Ka Sai always became arrogant when she was happy, that didn't change one bit. Of course, the bouquet flew towards me. In the nick of time, a girl threw herself in front of me and caught the bouquet. Everyone cheered, and that was when Ka Sai saw me. We stared at each other, just like eight years ago. I couldn't believe that I was there at her wedding. Didn't we fall out years ago? I walked towards them, and Ka Sai grabbed my hands. She introduced me to her husband as her best friend. Her husband shook my hand passionately, 'You must be Mei Ling!' North Eastern men had powerful hands. I smiled. The crowd gathered around the newlyweds once again. Ka Sai asked me to stay back after the wedding. Like before, I sat down without answering. Our reunion was much swifter and less awkward than I had imagined. I wondered what Ka Sai had told her husband about me, so that he could immediately recognise me.

I couldn't figure out how the seats were planned.

I wasn't allocated to the primary or secondary classmates' tables. I sat down at table B9. The lights dimmed and the newlyweds walked in. Rose petals rained down slowly from the ceiling. Although the restaurant exterior looked outdated, the hall inside was filled with a European aroma. I didn't really hear Ka Sai's speech. The falling petals reminded me of a scene from eight years ago, right before our falling out. It was summer, and we were standing under a Flamboyant tree in Kowloon Park. You said a lot of words to try to calm me down. You said you had fallen in love with a sailor and were going to sea with him for three years, and our Tibet trip had to be cancelled. You kept saying how I was the only one who understood you and loved you, but I couldn't hear a word you had said after hearing the words 'trip cancelled'. All I could see were petals of Flamboyant flowers falling on your head.

Flamboyant rose Flamboyant rose

Flowers.

There was a man's voice next to me. 'You are Chan Mei Ling?' I looked at the man, then looked at the screens around me playing photos of me and Ka Sai when we were young. The man looked at the pictures, then at me. He took a drink, and asked me to drink. When I didn't respond, he kept drinking. His arms were full of tattoos. I saw waves, I saw roses. I think he was the sailor Ka Sai had been talking about. She said his name was Marco. It was actually quite amazing that Marco was there, next to me. People say sailors are players. That's not true, he was getting drunk because of her. I grabbed a glass and then his bottle of XO. I thought, Jeez, who drinks XO nowadays? I wanted to drink some. The dishes kept coming, but we didn't touch the food. We just drank and drank. I began to lose focus, but I could see a man and a woman walking towards me. I grabbed Marco and ran out. I think he was surprised by my strength. I then passed out.

I let my body drift in the wind. I could hear his breathing, and the sound of ocean waves.

I smelled smoke. I opened my eyes and saw a yellowish ceiling. Marco had his back turned, smoking a cigarette. 'You're awake.' He said gently. I sat up nervously. He smiled, 'It's been a while since you've been to a hotel with a man?' 'What are you talking about? How did you know I am Mei Ling?' My attitude towards him was really quite bad. 'I know you just as you know me.' I should hate Marco, since he was the reason behind Ka Sai and my falling out. But he was so honest and straight that I put my guard all the way down. Since the moment I left my office to come to the wedding, I had not been calm for one second. Lo Wu, Guangzhou East Station, mud, stares, misty roads, Ka Sai's voice, reunion ... it all came back to me, each step heavier than the last. I had never seen falling out with Ka Sai as a major event in my life. It was always just a chapter, just like all the chapters. This was the first time I had directly faced our breaking off. Without this reunion, I don't think I would even realise how many years it had been. It would have just been a crack, forever forgotten.

'Why did you guys fall out?' Marco asked, next to me.

'I didn't, I just never contacted her again.'

'What's the difference?'

Marco seemed to me, all of a sudden, to encompass a bit of feminine compassion.

'So why did you break up with Ka Sai?' I looked at Marco's gentle eyes.

'I didn't, she just never came back to the ocean.'

His hands were shaking as he talked, and so too were the waves on his arm. Ka Sai had always been like that, doing whatever she wanted. She never went back to the mountains, either. We had spent most of our youthful days either at school or in the mountains. We loved hiking and dancing in the mountains. I loved watching her dance. At that moment, Ka Sai was right there, sitting opposite the two of us. She listened to our conversation in silence. I was a bit tired, so I leaned on Marco. He took me inside his ocean. We didn't say a word all night. We just listened to each other's waves and breathing.

That night
I saw the rose drifting on the waves
I saw the Flamboyant flower drifting on the waves
I saw …

FAB red vintage tea dress 1940s L@@K

Katie Popperwell

Beautiful red 100% silk vintage tea dress with gold ginkgo leaf pattern. Probably 1940s? VG vintage condition. Slightly frayed at the hem and with some wear at back of skirt. Grab a bargain!

A series of underexposed images showed a dressmaker's dummy at various angles, her hollow headless torso upholstered in dampish paisley, pictured against a brick wall. The dress draped over her frame belonged at a garden party with a curled head, ivory skin and perfect décolleté. Beatrice wasn't in the market for any of that. She didn't get invited to parties – not since they'd arrived here. She didn't go in much for dresses anyway, and her cropped, bleached hair was cut too short to hold a curl. She squinted at the screen and enlarged the picture to zoom in on the fabric, examining it for evidence of depth to reveal the quality of the silk. She resisted a twitch in her fingers as she imagined stroking the lustrous fabric, rubbing the pad of her thumb over the velvety softness and feeling the faint sticky resistance as her dry skin caught against the nap. They called it the 'queen of fibres' didn't they? She'd read that somewhere. Old silk always carried a very particular smell like rancid cod liver oil, the addictive odour of decay hinting at its origins in the guts of a worm.

She didn't want it, wasn't going to buy it. What would she do with it anyway? It probably wouldn't fit. Her tongue began to feel dry and her cheeks a little warm as her pulse began to quicken. Four bids already.

Time left: 2d 04h (24 May, 2015 06:37:12 BST)

6:37 AM Sunday morning. The username of the current high bidder was *scotslass77*. Beatrice wondered what kind of person would want a dress like this, what kind of person would want it so much that she had already placed a bid this early on. She conjured a slim girl in her early twenties; pretty with thick dark hair cut in to a heavy fringe, the kind of girl that might go to casual mid-week dinner parties with friends, have a creative job, maybe even a high-flying career; the kind of girl that was verging on gawky in secondary school but then really grew into her looks; the kind of girl that would joke around comfortably with male colleagues, safe in the knowledge that she was clever and charmingly quirky, but not so sexy so she made people uncomfortable. It wasn't that kind of dress. She had a steady boyfriend, but they wouldn't live together, she was too independent, and young – why would she want to be tied down so early when you thought about it?

No. Not that. Perhaps she was thinking of breaking up with him, perhaps that's why she wanted the dress, to wear on her first night out with the girls, her friends, they would be so giddy that she was single again, on the shots in some basement dive bar, you know what that lot are like … The front door opened, Beatrice closed the browser window, shut down the computer and went into in the kitchen.

Time left: 1 day 02 hours (24 May, 2015 06:37:12 BST)
6 bids

Two more bids and *scotslass77* still the high bidder. Beatrice ran her hands down her thighs, pressing down hard on a fresh purple bruise, and took in the remains of their evening; the glass rings on the table, the pile of dishes, the upended vase. A can had tipped over on the floor, leaked its gluey juice onto her magazine, swelling the pages, distorting the bodies of soap stars into pulpy ripples. The clean, static glare of the screen drew back her gaze. The dress was prettier than she remembered, the colour richer than before. The fabric tumbled around legless air in ripples and waves worthy of classic sculpture, the hypnotic geometry of the pattern was alive with the gentle pulsing of the screen. She scrolled down to the bottom of the page.

Q: Is there any size info on label? If not could you measure waist pls?
A: Waist measures 26in. flat. Label faded.

scotslass77 would have a 26in waist. She wasn't curvy, she was tall and willowy, some people probably said behind her back that she was too thin and made concerned faces like they were worried about her but really they were just envious. People always say that about bony girls, say they're too thin then fawn over their jutting collarbones. She'd probably lost weight too because of the boyfriend; all her friends would be saying she looked great. She'd smile and lower her eyes and say, 'Heartbreak diet!' with a pathetic little shrug. She'd be fine though, because she'd got that sort of self-assurance where it didn't seem to matter what she looked like. It did matter though, Beatrice knew that. She loved it really – you just knew she did. She could wear whatever she wanted and look gorgeous, and she wanted this dress, but she wasn't going to get it. The dress belonged to Beatrice, and no fake, ditzy anorexic bitch was going to take it away from her. She clicked the 'place bid' button and set her maximum bid at a price higher than she could afford. An uneven number, so that *scotslass77* would never guess it. She held her breath while she waited for the machine to respond, eyes fixed on the screen. She could feel her heart beating fast, alive and fierce.

You are the current high bidder

The red dress was alight with desire.

Spent, Beatrice turned off the computer. The empty screen became a mirror and she turned away. Looking down at the elasticated waistband of her pyjama bottoms she pushed her index finger sharply into the almost visible bump that was beginning to emerge from the folds of flesh around her middle and felt the hardness there that would not go away. She moved her fingers around her waist then along her arms, hugging herself, digging her nails into the flesh. Pulling her thick towelling dressing gown around herself she went upstairs and got into bed, tensing her abdomen and willing gravity to pull in her tummy as she lay on her back. He rolled over and hooked his arm tight around her. That night she dreamt of a girl with too-long legs and stars in her hair. She was dancing, spinning, laughing wildly in a red silk dress.

Beatrice woke up alone, sweating, wrapped up in too many layers and feeling sick. In the bathroom she stuck her fingers down her throat and felt better. Letting her rank, heavy clothes fall to the floor, she stepped into the shower and closed her eyes as the hot water streamed across her body. Lost in steam, she cradled an intense need for the red dress and the woman who would never have it. *scotslass77* would be rifling through her wardrobe, desperate for something to wear, and end up in a cheap modern dress made of synthetic fabric while Beatrice would be effortlessly chic and alluring in her one of a kind vintage treasure. The silk would slip over her thighs and belly like hot liquid, melting away all her imperfections to reveal the true Beatrice. Witty, confident and sexy, she could be all these things if only she had the right chance, the right life. She opened her eyes, turned off the shower and sat down on the edge of the bath, towel-swathed, watching steam condense on the cold window, trickle down and form a shallow, dirty pool along the sill.

Time left: 12m 29s Today 6:37AM
9 bids

The sky was still dark as she made her way downstairs on Sunday morning. Sitting at her computer in those final moments, Beatrice could almost feel the other girl, sitting at her own laptop, planning, calculating, looking at the same image on a different screen. It was all there to be decided, whose desire was the strongest, who was the smartest, the fastest, the most deserving of the prize. The screen remained static, except for the changing digits tracking the move toward zero hour. Beatrice, taut and awake, kept her eyes fixed and with four minutes to go was seized with panic. What if she was waiting right until the last minute? What if she had guessed at her highest bid? It suddenly didn't seem such a clever number after all. Beatrice bid against herself again and again and again, the number of bids changed from 10, to 11, to 12. No other bidders. Then it was over.

Congratulations! You won the item!

She screwed up her eyes and shuddered with joy, clapped the air, shut down the browser and went to the garden to sneak a cigarette before the day began.

The dress arrived on Tuesday morning, wrapped in a plastic bag inside a reused brown padded envelope. Beatrice let the parcel sit in her hand, measuring the weight of it before sliding her finger along the sellotape seam and letting the dress fall in to her lap. The stitching was beginning to loosen under the arms, and it was more patchy and faded than the former owner had admitted. The colour was a dark orange that made Beatrice think of her grandmother's scratchy seventies G-Plan couch. She picked up the shreds of discarded paper and plastic from the floor carefully and carried the remains of the parcel upstairs. She hung the dress in her wardrobe on a grey plastic hanger. Leaving the wardrobe door open and sitting on the end of the bed her gaze lingered on the crowded row of tattered dresses hanging before her. The light from the screen illuminated dusty rainbows of faded pinks, reds and greens in silk, taffeta and cotton, a phantom chorus line of unlived lives, empty husks, no less cruel for their stillness.

Beatrice took out her scissors and began to cut.

1961

Greg Thorpe

NEW YORK, APRIL 22, 1961

I decided I ought to quit my job after attempting courtship with a young woman who worked for the company. We had been on a number of dates and were soon the talk of the typing pool which I found to be unbearable and so I took to standing alone in the bathroom stalls for as long as I reasonably could at various points of the day. The girl was forward, a New York girl. Her kisses were wet and designed to encourage. She touched my leg in a bar where the bartender watched us with an unusual amount of interest. His sleeves were rolled up neat to the elbow showing forearms exotically brown against a pristine white shirt. He mixed a martini too dry and observed me as I drank it. The girl reminisced about high school and such as I dutifully lit her cigarettes.

For our final date together I had shown up drunk. I believe I was unkind. The girl ran down the street away from our rendezvous point outside the movie theatre. I immediately stumbled into traffic and hailed a cab that took me downtown where I was refused entry into a bar. A guy dressed mostly in white approached and said he knew of a place nearby where his friend worked the door and a guy like me might get a drink without any trouble. I followed him a little ways down the street and onto a quieter side street where he suddenly turned to face me. He held my jacket lapels with both hands and pulled me in. My blood began to pound. One hand was on my chest and into my jacket. He found my wallet, lifted it without a fight and in a couple of quick moves he popped the back of my knee and dropped me on the sidewalk. When I opened my eyes he was gone. I lay there a while listening to the rats.

I decided I would live downtown and after that a lot more drinking started to happen. One night I slept under trees in Central Park after sending my cab in the wrong direction. (I forgot I had a new address and ran short of money to pay the driver). I was too far gone to make it home on foot so I swerved my way three blocks to the park instead. Sometime in the night I woke from sobriety and the cold. I could smell cigarette smoke all around me but saw nobody.

The new apartment is a little cheaper and a lot smaller and anyhow I never mind starting over. Soon I will be twenty six years old. I have never made any plans except to come to New York City. In the new apartment I have clothes and records and a record player and shelves awaiting their books. Whatever else I owned has been returned to the collection of deserted city trash, going round and round, apartment to apartment, trying to find a place to fit.

I'm on Sixth Avenue and I jaywalk to Radio City Music Hall as a man is leaving the building. We look at one another on cue as if someone has sounded a bell. For a chilly morning he seems underdressed in white shirt with a jacket under his arm but soon I am close enough to notice that his forehead is glassy with sweat. I speculate that he works backstage at Radio City and for a second or two we are walking side by side in the same direction but he takes the lead and I slow a little and twice he looks over his shoulder to meet my eye as I fall into step behind him.

A little further along the street and he stops and turns. I instinctively go for my wallet which I have yet to replace.

'Excuse me sir,' he asks, 'do you happen to know the time?'

'I'm afraid I forgot to wear my watch today,' I reply.

'That's too bad.' He stays right where he is. The sweat is evaporating from his skin. My guess is he was making a delivery to Radio City and was late but now his errand is done.

'Are you late for something?' I ask. 'I'm pretty sure I'm running late myself. I have an interview this morning, all the way downtown.'

'I see. Good luck with that,' he laughs. 'I live midtown. Nearby. I guess I'll find out the time there.'

He stares at me and my mouth dries.

'Two guys without a watch, huh?' he continues through my silence. 'If you need to know the time right away, you could stop by my place I guess. It's real close.'

In the hallway of his apartment it is cold but warm at the same time and I hold my breath for too long and study the top of his head with the perfect parting in his hair and a crescent of shine from his pomade. When I reach to touch the side of his face my jacket sleeve pulls back and my watch face is caught in the meagre light.

When I return to the sidewalk shaking, I promise myself I will be here at the same spot at the same time at Radio City Music Hall tomorrow on Sixth. I walk all the way downtown, look nobody in the eye, miss the interview, go to a bar.

At home I am sorry to discover a full bottle by the bed, and one that's half empty. I drink shots and play a record but it was a mistake to arrive here empty handed. There is nothing to keep me home for long. The music puts me in the mood for a bar. Not company, just a bar. The Scotch puts me in the mood for company. I don't know the neighbourhood so I walk the streets smoking cigarettes. I pass a bar twice and as I finally go to enter, men begin to pour from the doorway and disperse on the street. The last guy to leave pulls a hat down over his eyes.

'No,' he says. 'Cops.'

A few blocks away now and this same guy is paying for our drinks. I guess he is ten years my senior. He wears a sharp cologne. He is easy enough to get along with. Even without the suit and the superior hat and the cologne I would guess he had money, the way he holds your eye, firm like a handshake. We have some laughs. My mind occasionally slips back to the hallway and the crescent of shine and it puts a pain in me so I finish the beer and switch to Scotch.

I know he doesn't live in the city and I want to know what has brought him to New York. He shows me a hotel room key and asks if I recognise the place. He isn't subtle but I'm too drunk for subtle so I ask again what brings him here and he tells me business.

'I have tickets for a show while I'm in town. Would you like to join me?'

'I'm too drunk for shows. I'd fall asleep.'

He laughs. 'Not tonight, tomorrow.'

'Don't you wanna bring your wife?' I look at his wedding ring.

'Chicago's a long way to come for a night, even for a show like this one.'

'Yeah, I guess.'

'We're having fun, right? Come to the show. You're busy tomorrow?'

'I'm never busy. Except when I am.'

'So we'll meet back here tomorrow night?'

I finish the whiskey and offer the empty glass to him without a word, like a kid waiting for milk.

'What if I change my mind?' I don't mean this to come out like a threat but it seems to.

'Then you can call me at …'

'There's no telephone where I live.'

'Then I guess you either don't change your mind or I go to the show alone.'

'I'll meet you back here.'

'Seven. We'll eat after the show.'

'I didn't say eat. It'll be late, tomorrow's Sunday, I got a new job starts Monday.'

'Great, we'll eat early.'

'I'll meet you at seven.'

'Seven. Okay.'

'Uh-huh.'

He pauses before ordering me another whiskey.

'I don't suppose you'd like a nightcap at the hotel ...'

'You suppose right.'

I drink the whiskey in one slug and walk out through the door of the bar and onto the street. A second later I hear music again as the door of the bar opens. I feel him watching my back. He's okay though. He's alright. I didn't ask what the show was. Tomorrow at seven.

NEW YORK, APRIL 23, 1961

A kid is screaming overhead. I shave and go to the corner for coffee, ditching bottles in the garbage wrapped up in newspapers like a baby I didn't ask for. I eat and I stand out on the corner, looking as far as I can along the curved street. I picture myself falling off a white building I have seen up in midtown and the thought takes some of the pressure off my chest. On Mulberry I collect a newspaper and I go to Columbus Park.

On a seat there I remember the night before. The glass, the ring, the cologne. I regret showing up drunk for my date with the girl from the office. I could have stayed at the job. It was something. I don't know what to do about it now. I will get a new position, make amends, work hard, participate. I will decide on the prettiest girl. I will notice.

Back in the apartment I stand in a nowhere part of the room. I turn around a couple of times, looking at nothing in particular. I say *'Hello'* out loud and test the sound of my voice. I have no telephone and I haven't told anyone that I moved. I think about where I might have seen a payphone. I don't know the neighbourhood, only a little in the dark. I don't know the payphones. I don't know what to do about it. I don't know what to do about any of it.

I sleep a little and get to the bar at six. He is in the same seat wearing a better suit than the night before, a better suit than me.

'I guess we could've dined together after all,' he says, more jokey than disappointed. 'Okay?'

He hands me a beer. I don't know what 'Okay?' means so I say, 'I ate. Sorry.'

'Don't be. I ate too.' He looks me up and down and his smile never breaks.

'I didn't know what I should wear,' I tell him. 'I mean, you never said where we were headed.'

'It's fine. You look okay. Really you do.'

'How come you're so early?' I ask. The beer is good but makes me hungry. I wish I really had eaten.

'How come you're early yourself?' he asks. His smile is annoying but also calms my nerves. He seems younger and brighter than the night before. He moves around a lot in his chair. If he didn't smile so much I would guess he was mad with me but why would he be mad? I decide maybe he's nervous and the idea makes me feel okay. The warm cold hallway and the white building and the crescent of shine come and go.

'I couldn't sleep so I just came along,' I tell him.

'Sleep? But it's 6:00 PM.'

'Yeah, well.'

'You wanna know why I'm so early?'

'I wanna know.'

He takes a sip of beer. 'Honestly? I had nowhere better to go.'

He laughs. I laugh.

We're about to leave for the show. I'm in the washroom at the bar. I stand by the basin for as long as I can. I'm not waiting but I'm expecting it. I feel the bulk of him arrive in the doorway behind me and his cologne arranges around me like smoke. I feel the warmth of a hand a little before it reaches the back of my neck. I know he can take care of whoever comes in. The squeeze comes a little harder and I suppose I would like to sleep, just like this, standing. 'It's okay,' he says. He holds my head from behind with the soft part of his thumb under my ear.

I show my city smarts by hailing a cab but then I go dumb when I remember I don't know where we're headed.

'Fifty-Seventh and Seventh,' he tells the driver.

'You guys are going to … ?'

'*Quiet!* Please, sir. Sorry, but this is a surprise for my friend here.'

'Okay, no problem. It'll sure be a surprise.'

'Fifty-Seventh and Seventh?' My mind moves through the streets ahead of the taxi cab. 'Carnegie?'

'Shoot,' he says, punching his palm, pretend mad.

'That's your surprise over, buddy,' says the driver. 'You don't know who's playing tonight though, huh?'

'Bernstein? Belafonte?'

'Enough!' says the guy and the driver laughs.

Less than thirty minutes later I am in the foyer of Carnegie Hall watching society enter through the door.

The guy returns from checking our coats. 'Okay?' My suit stands out a mile. Guys everywhere looking at guys everywhere. Guys looking at me then looking at him. That I cannot stand.

I tell him I prefer the aisle seat. It's maybe twenty minutes later when Judy Garland walks onto the stage, a tiny person from where we're sitting, only it doesn't matter because something happens to the air in the room so that it doesn't really matter where you are. The singing starts up and pushes everything right to the front of me. When You're Smiling is the song and once the music begins people either barely look at one another or else they can't stop and they pull at each other's sleeves like children.

Down on the stage she sings for so long that I mistakenly think the interval is the end of the show. On the staircase he says to me, 'Fine fine voice. I would've been here alone if not for you.'

I know it isn't true but I take it anyway.

'We could see another show,' he says. 'Perhaps next month?'

'All the way to New York just for a show? They don't have concert halls in Chicago?'

'The show would be one reason.'

Back in the auditorium the seats have grown too warm and his cologne is filling my chest right through That's Entertainment! which cuts my thoughts in two each time they happen. I feel him take a look at the side of my face. The chords are suddenly too much for me. I need everything to slow down. Slow down or be nothing at all. The next time I feel the edge of his finger touch mine it's during You're Nearer and it's a stupid game to play and I say *'Fuck you'* to myself and then *'Get off me'* right into his ear. Then he doesn't move a muscle for several minutes, cough, nothing. The music is too much and the tiny silences between the notes are too much and everything is right up in the front of me. Judy Garland is singing If Love Were All and at the edge of my sight I feel his chin raise a fraction. I imagine the landing of my fist across his jaw and I imagine the white building over in midtown, and the hallway, the wallet, the movie theatre, the girl, the martini, all of it running in the wrong order.

The more you love a man,
the more you put your trust,
the more you're bound to lose.

I'm out of my seat and gone.

JUNE 22, 1969

I walk into my kitchen and pluck Jeremiah from his chair and place him on my knee to negotiate breakfast. With sticky palms he slaps at the newspaper on the table in front of him where the words read:

Judy Garland Dead At 47.

'Jeez,' I say, my breathing gone a little. 'Jeez.' I squeeze the boy to me.

Over my shoulder my wife reads and says, 'I know. God. It's too bad. Those poor kids.'

'I heard her sing once.'

'Really? When you lived in New York?'

'Yeah.'

'Wow. You never told me that.'

'Carnegie Hall.'

'No kidding? Jeremiah, honey, don't tear up the newspaper, daddy's reading.'

I press my face into Jeremiah's hair and it blots out the sound of her singing, and the smell of cologne.

White Nights

JUDITH BARRY

He is lying on the couch, the book still open. The page is a bit smeared, not like the ink has run, and not dirty, but this page so often lighted upon by his fingers that the ink is faint and the paper is turning dark.

His wife, Irina, where is she? His great love, still so beautiful. He must have dozed.
He thinks, she must not have wanted him to know she was going.
How grey it is outside, and yet, he still hears birds.
The window is open.

He had been thinking and fell asleep.
It had all been so clear before. Not that anything had really changed. He was the same.
He did the same things. He felt as he always did. He

thought. What was different now, really nothing, nothing at all.

Before, when he had been anxious, he had not been so sure.
Or maybe, he wasn't sure *then* that what he was doing *now* was the right thing.
But now, with all that had happened, he knew that that time had been his to make use of for his work, for work which was respected then. More than that, accepted as being important. His life made sense then, even his anxiety. Now did it all still make sense to anyone other than him?

He gets up and goes to his desk. On the table are his notes, where he left them, beside the computer. He rereads what he had written. It's too late now to do more. Poetry is his life, it's all he has.

He looks in the mirror, he looks older now, he thinks … But it's time to meet Sasha.

The city is full … everyone is out and it's warmer than it was inside.
The sun glows red in his eyes. How different the day seems now.
He walks quickly.
Past the shops still open, longer now because of the daylight.
Past the church, across the square, and then he stops at the back of the hotel.

The sun glints against the long windows. He has always

wanted to stay at this hotel. It was one of a very few built in the 70s, perfectly symmetrical from all sides, meant as an improvement on palace architecture or maybe a condemnation – he isn't sure of the intent any more. But the hotel was never completed, and now, parts are crumbling. Even with a thousand rooms still in service, some of the floors are closed off. He now sees how the sun hitting the windows turns the empty stories into dashed lines.

He considers cutting through the back entrance as a faster way to the front, but sees the lines, cars and then people, both single file, waiting …
And he has to be on time.

In front of the hotel, the long windows are solemn, they don't omit light, black teeth in a mouth too big to ever break into a grin.
Are the street lights on yet, no? Still too early.
There is electricity? Yes, he hopes.

He hurries up the long steps and rushes into the lobby toward the huge baronial desk.
His cousin is already there.

Sasha looks rumpled and a bit swallowed by his suit – it's seersucker, so wrinkled that it's hard to distinguish the stripes in the pattern among all the creases. His hair is lanky and matted, but still blond. And his face is still delicately beautiful, even now.

'Welcome cousin,' Sergei says, and they hug.
'Did you have a good journey?'

Sasha sighs, 'Yes, yes it was fine, but we have now just checked in as the room was not ready (laughs). Some things are still the same.'
'It is so kind of you to bring us here.'
'If we weren't so cramped for space you might have stayed with us … but I thought it would be better for Anna if you stayed here, as you will appear more autonomous, and we can look in on you as well.'

'Yes this is better. The room is big, so we are fine.'
Sasha goes to slap Sergei's back, but then thinks better of it, and puts his hands in his pockets.

'Rudolph and Gustov send their love and ask after you,' he continues, 'and want to visit you someday, too. Of course, only if there is something to be done with them.'
His face brightens into an enormous smile at the thought.

Sergei looks mildly uncomfortable at the mention of the two boys, but he tries not to show it.

'I have to go to the others now,' he says, 'to be sure they are all coming. You, Anna and Veronika must be at the park by 10:00 PM tonight. Don't be late.
I will meet you at the entrance, there is only one.
Please say my hellos and welcomes to Anna and Veronika.'

Sergei starts to turn to leave, 'Oh, and did they,' looking towards the hotel concierge, 'give you the dress I left? Irina picked it out.'

'Yes, yes and it is beautiful and fits Anna perfectly … How did she know it would fit her? She is a vision.'

'I can't wait to see her,' Sergei says, and then he hugs his cousin again, and rushes away.

As Sacha watches Sergei leave, his expression grows more serious as though he is only just now realising the importance of this evening and what he hopes will be its logical and longed for conclusion.

Around 9:00 PM Sasha, Veronique, and Anna make their way to the park. Petersburg is now glowing in the soft light of the falling sun. As they make their way, Sasha wonders that the city still has almost no signage. It is up to the people and the buildings reflecting in the endless summer light to render this scene, he realises with a smile.

The Nevsky is crowded … old women in babushkas, some selling food, others sitting, some begging, and cursing, and East Russian traders, their colourful clothing adding to the festive air, and still-employed proles in their work clothes, making their way home, some with empty bags, and farmers from the countryside dressed in their best clothes – Sasha can tell they have come for their monthly provisions, and Finns standing out with their white blond hair, and tourists everywhere … English words melding into Japanese, alongside German, Finnish, French, Italian, Chinese, Arabic and some he does not recognise. And so many men, most of all he is aware that there are many men on the street, many men in business suits, and many more men than women. Although he is able to pick out some young women, too, in all sizes, some walking alone, and others in a group that look like they might be their families. Everyone seems dressed as though for a party. It will be a party, Sasha imagines, a party to celebrate the longest night of the year.

Heads turn to look at Anna, and pride overtakes him as they walk along the Prospect. She is glorious in her diaphanous summer dress. Her golden hair curling slightly around her face, blending with the cascade of subtle colours that catches the light and everyone's eyes as she moves. He hadn't realised how tall she would be in her high heels. Her legs are so long and how did she learn to walk so well? Yes, he thinks, she is stunning.

They enter the park. For Sasha it seems as though they have entered onto a stage.
The park has street lamps that emit a bright yellow light, creating yellow shafts as it connects with the fog coming up from the water, and illuminating the park unevenly.
Suddenly, he remembers the first poetry reading of Sergei's he attended.
It was in a large room not so far from here, an old ballroom in an early nineteenth-century mansion. The room was so crowded he had to stand. Sergei, so elegant, so handsome, stood on a small platform. As he read, he barely looked at his manuscript. He spoke with such emotion that Sasha was surprised to find that he was affected by every word, his eyes wet, and he was crying. Thinking about it now, he couldn't recollect what the poem was about, but he

could vividly recall the contagion of Sergei's passion, and it was that passion that had produced corresponding emotions in him. He had not felt that way in a long while.

He sees Sergei, still elegant, already there in the park, talking to some men standing near a bench in back of the wide path that skirts the river. These men look to be different ages.
Some in their late twenties, early thirties, while others might be as old as Sasha and Sergei, over forty … and a couple look even older. Altogether he counts ten. They are all dressed up for the occasion, he realises, as though they are going to a fancy dress ball, so this must be the group. Sergei hasn't told him much about them, just that they are well-to-do, and that they are eager.

Looking around he notices that most of the wooden benches in the park are occupied, and by families. A mother, a father, even a grandmother, and sometimes a few young children. All sit single file on these benches. He looks over to where Sergei is standing and he sees that there is an empty bench about eight feet behind the bench where Sergei is standing with the men. But then he understands that the bench isn't really empty. There is a picnic hamper occupying the centre, and he has seen it before.
Of course, that bench is for him, and for Veronika.

Sergei comes over to Anna, Sasha and Veronika.
He embraces Veronika, and glancing at Anna, says, 'I always wanted to travel back in time, and you two', he looks at Sasha, 'have made that possible.'

'Look at her,' indicating Anna, 'If I didn't know better I would think she was you when we were young.' He hugs Veronika again, and then puts his arm gently around Anna.

Anna looks at him. Her face is so innocent, he thinks. She has her mother's high wide forehead and turquoise flecked brown eyes. Anna looks at her parents trying not to show any expression. She wants this night to be perfect for them. It must be everything that everyone wants it to be. She is so happy, to be here, away from the farm, out of the country, and in this magical city which now seems like something she has always dreamt of. And now it is about to become true.

Sergei is talking to her. He says, 'You are like a butterfly that has emerged from its cocoon tonight. You are the most beautiful girl here.'
Sergei looks in the direction of the wide path along the river. Already there are many young women, elegantly dressed, promenading slowly along the path in both directions.
'Come, my butterfly … I want you to shine,' he says. 'So many here are waiting for you.'

Sergei takes her arm and escorts her to the path. And she begins her walk.
And indeed, she does shine that night and all her dreams become real.

Years pass.
A woman looks out an open window in another city, a city not Petersburg.

It is the city where she went to live out the promises of that night. She thinks back on that night. She imagines Sergei, and her parents on the Nevsky, and when she does this, it is once again, that night, White Nights. And the evening unfolds all over again. She replays it all again.

And she wonders about Irina, Sergei's wife. Where is she now?
She never appeared during that long night, that long night of walking, where she walked and walked in her diaphanous dress. While her parents, and sometimes Sergei, sat on the bench. Watching her, and watching different men approach her, to talk for a while.
Her parents stayed on that bench all night, watching her. Sergei was always watching her, too, watching everything from many directions. He kept track of the men, to see who they were, and he looked to her parents for their reactions, and he paid close attention to her, to her expressions, even though she was trying not to show any.

And then, every so often, he would look over expectantly toward the entrance to the park.
It must have been to see if Irina would appear. But Irina never arrived. Not even at dawn after the bridges that had been raised in celebration of that night, closed again, not even as the city returned to its normal state. Irina did not come to see Anna in the park that night. She never returned.

It is getting cold. Anna closes the window and walks to the back of the room.

All around her are many boxes and it looks like she is packing. She opens a door. It is a closet. Inside, the closet is nearly empty. Hanging by itself, on a hanger, is the diaphanous dress she once wore.

Don't snazz my twinkle. Ever. – Multiverse report #88

AL AND AL

In present time, I am lurking on the corner of Whitworth Street West, Manchester. A boy dressed in white is running across the street under the railway arches shouting, '*We are the children of the future.*' Candle shadow bodies evaporate in the echo. It is 1988. The double 8 in 88 is causing a spectral infinity loop in the Multiverse Map. The Map connects soul mates. This is the first time I am destined to meet him. As he stands alone at the corner, my double waves sadly from the Street of Chance. Film union shy spirit couldn't find the content. Atoms nervously vibrate together. Everyone notices him. He is shining on the inside. Glowing like a prince. He does not walk around the yacht-builder's yard, he glides and hovers on the podium, like a new God incarnate. I am going to miss this opportunity to meet him. Teenage excuses abandon steely will. The Multiverse will have to find another way to connect us. A detention in time.

As I write this I look up at the television; the screen is showing me an English Governess in a Siamese Court. It's 1861, but the film's simulation is opulent in the vibrant colours of a 1956 drama. After the English school teacher has met the King's 82 children she is taken to her bedroom. All 39 of the King's wives and concubines are giggling at her Victorian shape, they want to see underneath her massive dress. 'Does she have legs?' She pulls up her hooped skirt and begins singing about her dead husband ...

Hello young lovers, whoever you are,
I hope your troubles are few.
All my good wishes go with you tonight,
I've been in love like you.

Be brave, young lovers, and follow your star,
Be brave and faithful and true,
Cling very close to each other tonight.
I've been in love like you.

I know how it feels to have wings on your heels,
And to fly down the street in a trance.
You fly down a street on the chance that you meet,
And you meet – not really by chance.

This lady knows the street of chance is a rigged wheel. When chance meetings occur, soul mates locate each other on the Map. This King is obviously an expert Map reader. Love is in the air at his palace. In my house there are many mansions. The Map is a projection representing the lines of latitude and longitudinal forces in the Multiverse. Maps were originally created to position us on earth. The landscape was drawn up to be a mirror of the constellations. The Map connected us to the heavens. The Multiverse Map is a search engine for love. Every possible time space path is taken to find love. It is not good for man to be alone. In Heartbreak Hotel you get so lonely you can die. Storm the simulated reality and retake the Multiverse. You can only do this with the correct accomplice. It is written in the Map. There is always some way of getting where you want to go. Learn to think in association blocks and see the instructions conveyed, your collaborators will appear. Through the time projector, infinite potential becomes solid. Study all the signs reality is showing you, and watch the reality film quiver under close examination. The new High Priests in Physics see atoms gazing back at us. A seductive atomic glance turns away and hides when it notices our scopophilic stare is watching, shy to reveal all its secrets. Derek said, *'Time is what keeps the light from reaching us'* …

It was in Derek's sweet garden of vanished pleasures the Map finally conjured the appointed hour we met. In the fisherman's prospect cottage, the atoms trembled in anticipation as we studied the nuclear power station induce a fission reaction. The dead artist had marked ley lines in the Dungeness shale with circles of magical stone. In Derek's Gethsemane and Eden I was flirting with my camera, creating ghost pictures that would never be seen. Blue butterflies, Sussex emerald moths flutter in my presence. I notice my soul mate standing weightless, his feet leave no impression in the shingle. He is naked except for a quiver of silver arrows and a bow, he radiates a calm disdainful authority. He speaks English to me. After he has spoken I know what

I must do. Up on the lighthouse balcony the dance of destiny signalled a path across the glittering sea. It was the ordained hour to reclaim my gills. Don't turn away from love, sailor. Being with the one is like walking on water, you just have to believe in the miracle. The canon lawyers could not stop this love affair. Like the legendary fishermen who discover the utopian landscape of the peach blossom spring, I had been living in the 16th century unaware of the passing of time. It was time to come down from reading in the autumn mountains and take my chances with my soul mate. Lick it and like it.

Mozart's 23rd Piano Concerto in A, Adagio is playing. I picture every detail of my lover's body. I know his beautiful ears. His long, slender, precise, talented fingers. Nails bitten. His petite nose I have studied in his sleep. Breathing. His dark chocolate eyes, full of light. All his teeth lined up perfectly next to one another, always ready to break out into a smile of mischief. A shared sketch. I stroke his abdominal ridges. Feel his ticklish tension under my delicate strokes as I move up to his nipples electrically connected to his glistening cock. Running from his scrotum up the centre of his arse hole is the most perfect seam. Dividing his left and right side like a ruler. I have never seen a more precise mark on flesh that has not been etched by a tattooist.

I cut his toe nails. I run hot water and bathe his feet in scented salts. His skin is sensitive to heat. My blood is red hot. I can heat a cold bed in less than a minute. In winter he jumps into bed, snuggling up to me like a block of ice, only retreating to his side as he begins to melt from contact. We have sides in bed. I'm on the left, he is on the right. When he snuggles, I face the outside of the bed and our bodies fit perfectly, locking together. I cannot remember how we established bed sides, but it was like this from the first night, over 6000 nights ago. We've slept together every night since. I wonder how many more nights we have together? Free from disease and certain death. And will we meet again some place, somewhere? In another place, in another time? Be together forever? I hope so. Love in the Multiverse, a special relativity. Where does our love go when we no longer have bodies to carry our thoughts and feelings? Albert says $E=mc^2$. Converting units of mass to units of energy. The speed of light. A black hole churning out another beginning, another end. Joseph wanted to abolish death.

Inside our greenhouse stocked with carnivorous plants. I sit on a railway sleeper with my soul mate. It's 90 degrees. We are watching insects be seduced by the plants. A lovely chrome blue bottle stops on the edge of a Venus flytrap. Just one more step and we will witness nature's macabre play of kinetic insect murder. SNAP! The trap doors close, 3 spikes hold the fly in position as the plant crushes the life out of it. In a few days the plant will re-open, the fly will be drained of its juices, its dry carcass left to rot in the sunlight. The plant waits for its next visitor, its next meal. Atoms eating atoms.

My soul mate started collecting carnivorous plants after we had a beehive in our studio roof. It was during the time scientists announced bee numbers had dramatically fallen, and therefore the whole ecological system was in danger of collapse. So we let the bees move in and left them to get on with pollinating our Universe. We can hear the buzzing drones above our heads inside the studio. When our computing machines are on, the sound of the beehive vibrates in perfect harmony. The bees communicate by dancing. The magical fortifiers guard the ravers. From the beauties and wonder of apiculturc we make jars of the sweetest honey dripping from the combs.

Andy says if you do something once it's exciting, and if you do it every day it's exciting. Nothing in between is as good as once or every day. Every day I make dinner for my soul mate. The dining table is dressed in white table linen. Candles burn at seven. Every day is a special occasion. We work and we play. From when we wake, to when we sleep. The menu rotates across the days. We stick our forks into super foods. Running a body, replenishing DNA, requires energy. And then you can never be certain all the cells are going to copy perfectly. After working at the nano scale, we postulate DNA will recognise the potential in Alan's new intelligent Thinking Machine species. IBM store binary code onto DNA, not long now before evolution instigates a potential future away from the earth bound animal plant kingdom and into deep space. An afterlife of machine bliss. Love letters in binary, travelling across the universe living happily ever after. Saying those three words forever ...

01001001 00100000 01101100 01101111 01110110
01100101 00100000 01111001 01101111 01110101

Will you marry me?

We once thought the answer would always be Till Death Do Us Join. But now we can do it. One day we will be equal lovers. Two coordinates immediately appropriate the drum of memory. An emerald ring is in process. I want you to be my receptacle. What does that involve? Everything dirty boy. Welding two brains and bodies together with vibrating feedback. The screen shapeshifted into a movie. I am composite now. Woke up with other thoughts and memories. Some of them mine, some of them his. Takes time to get used to it.

Sipping twinkle cocktails out of giant champagne saucer glasses in Spitalfields, London. The bubbles carry alcohol into the lungs, bypassing the liver and heading straight for the bloodstream. We are sat at a table eating fish and chips with comrades from HOME, the glass house for culture, on the second evening of its press launch. The dim memories of a car park that once stood beneath the foundations of this new risen HOME flicker in my mind. Stagnant glass smashed from car windows. Souvenirs of addiction sparkling on rubber tyres. My twinkle is sitting next to me now, sipping his twinkle. As he puts his glass down, the waitress mistakenly tries to take the drink away before he has finished. He stops her in mid motion and corrects her. Turning back to the table he exclaims, 'She tried to snazz my twinkle!' I look at him quizzically: Snazz? Omar tweets the moment, publishing the word. Sarah favourites it, confirming its existence. Looking back at the fizzing glass I see his cup is overflowing, because we have always known heart pounding love. A Gemini expedition with no hiccups. So don't snazz my twinkle. Ever.

The day before, we stood on a ley line together. Outside a partially built HOME. We were footsteps down the windy street from a long time ago, the light from faraway stars. HOME is the precise location where we began this story. On the corner of Whitworth Street West Manchester where I first saw my soul mate 27 years ago. Where image dust in space still sees the ravers flying out of the Haçienda, announcing the future. The contagion spread rapidly and changed the City for good. I remember the boy, 18, dressed in white, running across the street under the railway arches shouting, *'We are the children of the future.'* Candle shadow bodies evaporated in the echo. It was 1988. The spectral infinity loop in the Multiverse Map has connected us back to its origin. He's here with me now. The Map connects soul mates. That was the first time I was destined to meet him. And now, as we stand together at the corner, our doubles wave back at us from the Street of Chance nearly 30 years younger. Film union shy spirit found the content. Atoms vibrated together. Love shines on the inside. Glowing forever.

He Goes

JASON WOOD

Max had never been able to get over the endings of certain films. They dogged him for months, years even. Cinematic conclusions where the enduring possibility and affirmation of love was tentatively suggested only to then, at the death, be cruelly denied.

Woody Allen's monochrome *Manhattan* had been a long lasting fixation. A contrite Isaac, played of course by the director himself, unable to find a taxi and sprinting through the New York streets to try to persuade Tracy, a young Mariel Hemingway with cheekbones that could cut glass, not to board the flight to London that will take her away from him and bring down the curtain on their imperfect but nonetheless romantic stop-start affair.

Though initially open-minded, Max altered his stance and later opposed the view given by those of more optimistic natures who saw the ending as suggesting that love may well prevail after all and that distance and absence will prove to be surmountable barriers. 'Sometimes you just have to have a little faith in people,' intones Tracy in a surprisingly mature and soothing tone. Isaac cracks the briefest of smiles and allows himself to look briefly to the future and consider a time when they may be together again. After all, 'What's six months if we still love each other?' Cue Gershwin and a montage of New York skylines.

Max however now saw things quite differently. For him, the scene was like a guillotine. Tracy will go, and as Isaac earlier suggested, meet new men, and ones her own age, and move on with her life. There will be corruption. Maybe Tracy will also one day arrive at a crossroads of the heart, where she can dispense hurt and be hurt in return. But in that moment Max all too clearly understood, as no doubt Isaac did, that through his own, admittedly intermittently charming egotism, selfishness and prevarication, Isaac was guilty of squandering something potentially beautiful, potentially permanent and concrete. Of course, we can never really know. Beyond the world of the film things may well have ended badly for the couple. Affairs, children, debt, alcoholism, sexual dysfunction and finally a bitter and protracted custody battle. But for those final moments on screen Max willed Tracy not to get on the plane. To embrace Isaac. To stay.

And now there was a new obsession. Far worse even than the last. A film in which the tentative overture towards the possibility, however slim, of resurrection suggested by Woody Allen and Marshall Brickman was replaced by an emotionally crippling sense of finality.

Swayed by good reviews that hinted at a love story

with a potent whiff of Robert Graves' *Love Without Hope*, Max had first seen Andrew Haigh's *Weekend* on the cinema screen. As was his habit. He had gone alone. The tale of Russell and Glen, two gay men who meet at a pick-up club and then over the next forty eight hours slowly, and against all odds, become inseparable, completely crushed him. He went to see it seven times in two weeks. Always alone. The cinema staff began to eye him suspiciously and to make the odd sarcastic comment. In the end Max switched cinemas and was finally thankful when the DVD of the film came out some time later. When it did, there began an endless cycle of viewing and reviewing the final scenes. It became an addiction. A habit Max was unable and unwilling to break.

The affair depicted starts off as a bit of a lark, a mutually convenient transaction of desire in which two people ultimately discover that rather than just a quick but satisfying fuck there is a spark ignited between them that suggests a deeper connection and the possibility of two lost souls, though neither would perhaps think of themselves as such, who may have found something permanent and long-lasting in each other. The trouble is, one of the men, Glen, is going away at the end of the weekend and not just for six months. He is going away for far longer and to somewhere far further; Portland, Oregon.

When Max initially watched the film he was able to cope, though not with great comfort, with the sense that this was a relationship that was destined to burn brightly but for only a short period. To flicker, but then be distinguished by mutual consent. But in the course of the film something fatal occurs. Love raises its ugly head and despite their bravado, the pair realise that their parting, enforced as it is, is irreconcilable with their emotions.

Like a man stuck on endless repeat, Max found himself unable to recover from the final two scenes in the film. In the first, the two lovers part on a grey train station platform. They kiss goodbye, to a cacophony of insults from straight onlookers. There is no suggestion of writing, communicating in any way or of attempting to sustain the relationship. And all despite the twenty-first century ease of staying in touch. There is also no question that the trip, for the sake of love and perhaps a greater good, should be aborted. Glen boards the train. He does not hesitate. Not for a second. He goes. There is not even the attempt to persuade him to stay. Both men know the cause is lost. Max, who has personally never suffered any relationship angst but was just a soul in torment, living his life a little vicariously through culture, found the sense of absolute closure brutal and completely debilitating.

The closing scene is the unwrapping of the gift of a tape recorder. It's a little in-joke. In the recorder is the tape the two men made for an art project in which their first night of passion is recounted with candour. As Russell listens back to his own words, caressing the recorder whilst looking out from his high-rise apartment, dusk descends and with it an impending sense of solemnity. The film seems to want to suggest that despite the momentary loss and desolation life will go on. The sadness will pass.

Max knows otherwise and thinks back to the train leaving the station, thinks back to the weekend the characters enjoy. He thinks back to the dancing and the drinking. Thinks back to the kissing and the snogging. The sucking and the fucking. He thinks back. He goes. And now. He is gone.

The Elevated Woman

DECLAN CLARKE

The first time ever he climbed the steps it was to do the recce. He brought his nephew for cover. No one ever suspected young parents of anything, except perhaps of being a touch self-absorbed. That made sense. Anyone looking would focus on the child, not the accompanying adult. And any lazy police officer investigating afterwards would immediately rule out a young parent. Police were always like that. They believed in 'hunches' or 'gut feelings'. Gobshites – they were usually more interested in acting like police officers than doing any deductive policing. Or the ones he had met were, and he'd met enough of them.

There were 168 steps in all, two more than it said at the turnstile, not that he noticed. His nephew was too young and slow to walk all the way, or even a quarter of it. He carried him up 146 of the steps. When he got to the viewing platform he was sweating. A bright March sun was low in the sky and went straight into his eyes. He couldn't see anything. He wanted to get closer to the monument base, but a young couple were leaning against it, locked in a lecherous embrace. They clearly felt good about themselves, but the display seemed more about everyone else noticing rather than quenching their own urges.

'Gobshites,' he thought, 'just like a pair of cops.'

He noticed her foot first. It was far more elegant than he had expected as he first approached the monument base, and it focused his mind. He looked up at the statue. From his perspective he could see the contours of the slim robes the sculptor had chosen to preserve her sense of modesty in the portland stone.

'Enjoying the view are ya?'

It took a moment before he realised the young man was addressing him. He looked down. As he did so he caught a glimpse down the blouse of the girl. He saw plenty.

'Wh-at?' he said, quickly raising his eyes to meet those of, as he now realised, a late adolescent boy. The boy's eyes had a provoking glint that barely concealed the boundless stupidity that lounged behind them.

He paused.

'Nothing doing today,' he thought. He turned to his nephew. 'C'mon,' he said, 'keep hold of my hand.' They moved toward the stairwell, ignoring the young couple.

'Prick,' said the adolescent, as he began his descent with the child, but he didn't care.

He thought about her as soon as he woke up the next morning, but he put it out of his mind. He had too many other things to resolve first. His best idea, that of using a child as a distraction, was gone.

In fact, that was his only idea.

He got up, dressed, and went downstairs to get his breakfast. Tea, bread and butter. The knife he used was one he had taken from his mother's kitchen when he had visited a few months back. He liked how it spread the yellow matter across the rough white surface plain. Sharp knives were useless. His mother had noticed this absence as she had mentioned it the next time he had gone around. He wasn't sure if this was because she knew he had taken it, or because of her habit of airing her grievences aloud.

He still didn't know what he was going to do, and as he pondered this, he thought about her again. That was twice, and it was only twenty past eight.

The next time, he waited until a group of tourists had alighted from a bus and made their way to the entrance. He figured he'd blend in with them. Halfway through queuing he realised the attendant didn't give a shit who came in or out and wouldn't remember him if he came here daily with an arse for a face.

He found out all he needed to know that time. At the top of the rotunda on which the monument stood, at the opposite side to the doorway, was a ledge that would do the job. He'd have to wait until just before 6:30 PM, but, if he timed it right, it would probably work out fine. As he descended he thought about her breasts, and how they had looked in the sunlight that last time. A funny thought to have at this moment, but he had it anyway.

That evening, he went to meet his contact. He got there at a quarter to seven. His contact showed up at eight-thirty. He was sitting at his table when he got back from the toilet.

'All set?'

'All set.'

'Need anything extra?'

'No, what we discussed will be fine.'

'You know where to collect it?'

'I do.'

'Grand so.'

He nodded as his contact got up and left. He waited about twenty minutes, finished his drink, and then left himself. He thought about her again as he walked home.

He looked at the clock on the adjacent building as he turned the corner. It was quarter past six. He walked to the turnstile and paid entry. The attendant didn't look up, he only saw the reflective surface of the peak of her cap.

He moved slowly forward and began to walk up the stairs. This was the part he was most aprehensive about. Explosives could be temperamental, and the constant shifting of balance as he walked up the stairwell could easily trigger something. He tried to keep his back straight as he climbed the steps and made an effort not to sway to either side. After thirty six steps he began to feel a pain in the base of his spine and down the backs of his legs. He noticed he was clenching his teeth.

He paused three times on the way up, but when he walked out onto the viewing platform no one else was present. He stopped and looked out over the city. He didn't want to look up, and he felt light-headed. After a moment, he composed himself. He turned around and looked up at the monument. He picked out the smoothness of her face, and noticed that her eyes were looking towards the Post Office, and not, as he had thought, in the direction of the river.

He stuck his head back through the doorway to see if anyone was climbing the stairs. He heard nothing. He walked around the rotunda, and when he reached the ledge he took off his coat. He took the device out of the canvas bag he had hanging around his neck, and set the timer. He lifted it carefully onto the ledge, and had to stand on his toes to move it into position. He put his coat back on and moved back around the rotunda. As he reached the exit he looked up again.

When he was a short way down the stairs he turned suddenly and ran back up to the platform. He grabbed the edge of the device and flung it over the railing to the street below.

He saw the flash just before he heard the loud bang and the shattering of glass. Alarms went off immediately. The screams were at first isolated, but they grew in volume and mass as people ran to the pillar base.

A Summer Romance

Irina Gheorghe

I still can't remember the first time it became apparent. All I know is that it took over my mind with such speed, that a time preceding it became impossible to locate, even as a distant memory. I say it took over my mind not because I think it was actually happening in my mind, but more as a comforting strategy which might, if taken for granted, provide some sort of account for what was going on. Confining the inexplicable to the realm of the psyche seems to be the most efficient method to keep the world in its place, and that's just what I was encouraged to do. Just exile anything out of the ordinary into the untrodden lands of a disturbed mind, and that's the end of it. Things are safely where we know them to be, and this is all that matters.

And still, I am not at all convinced that it was actually in my mind. Rather, I would say that it was always around somewhere and its emergence into my life, rather than actual eruption from within, resembles much more a gradual, infinitesimal invasion, like the slow coming into focus of a previously blurred image which was there all along. Even now, when it is obstinately gone, I still retain a vague, indefinite impression that it is someplace close. And I keep looking with the fervour of fresh infatuation, retaining the hope that someday it will return.

However, if I was to decide on a beginning, it must have been one of those sunny days when I first started to explore the surroundings of my new abode. I wasn't used to the particularities of life there, and found it quite unusual. Nobody else seemed to notice the air of strangeness hovering over the place, and I first thought it was just a matter of habituation. And maybe it was, to a certain extent, but I never managed to grow used to it. The gloomy, rainy days were, oddly, less disturbing than the sunny ones. At the time it was impossible to pin it down but now, in the light of later developments, I can see why. The haziness of the clouds and fog, through their layers of rarefied matter imprecisely superimposed over the visible world, were subtly indicative of something that escaped the eye and, thus, more in keeping with a general sense that something was out of place. The blinding light of a summer afternoon, by contrast, was much more cunning and deceptive; it created the illusion of a perfect view, without washing away the eeriness. Something was out of place, but the shift had been imperceptible; the clear-cut boundaries of things in the harsh midday light had washed it all away.

So it must have been one of those bright days that it first occured to me that things were slightly different from how they used to be. It was the same as when someone grows old next to you, changing bit by bit, but you never notice because you are always there, until one day when you see an old photograph and it dawns on you that so much has changed.

We always think of change as something happening in time, encroaching time like a tentacular monster, unfolding it upon itself, cutting it violently with countless invisible blades like the merciless light cutting a sharp edge between the bright side and the shade. Why can't we imagine the same happening with space? For this is exactly what it was: something was taking over the space around with the patience of a smitten teenager driven by the faraway goal of persuasion.

If it did start somewhere, then it must have been around the homogeneous shapes spread in the area. They seemed to have the form of solid structures but the texture of organic mass, severed in perfect squares, circles and triangles. They gave a troubling uniformity to the whole place, and, however hard I forced my memory to remember them, they did not look familiar. And more than that, they were structuring the landscape as if they were following an invisible pattern, like a secret code puncturing the visible with hidden messages. At the beginning I was still putting it down to improper adjustment. I still was not used to that environment, which whatever I did retained a sense of the uncanny. But no, that wasn't it. Whenever I followed a certain path, I had a feeling I was being lead down it, and the strangest thing began to happen: all these shapes that appeared would just stay there, even if space had changed and my eyes could not perceive them anymore. They lay over each other to create more complex shapes. A triangle over another triangle and another one and another one until a very complex structure emerged, and then it froze. Together with space, time was becoming flat itself, instead of developing sequentially it advanced by accumulation, growing into a two-dimensional structure which would become fixed for a while.

As if this wasn't enough, structures started to repeat. Or was it the same one appearing at different times and places? Maybe it is better to say that it was absorbing time and place to accumulate into a manifestation of itself. At this stage my confidence that this belonged to the external world was for the first time seriously shaken. Was this not a mere hallucination of my mind gone off track? And yet, there was a chance of something actually being there, only making itself visible for me to see it. The most extraordinary thing.

Either way, I *did* want to see it again. From aimless wanderings my explorations turned into obsessive searches. I *had* to see it again. I started to look at everything not for what it was, but for the potential it had, with enough patience and movement, to develop into something else and reveal the marvellous thing I was looking for.

Strangely, I saw fewer and fewer people, as if the place was becoming deserted. One time, in one of the open green areas I was searching in, I came across a rectangular figure with a circular shape on top of it. Quickly I approached, full of hope and tenderness.

'Good afternoon!' I heard as soon as I came near.

It was the voice of my next door neighbour, but nothing of what I saw resembled her. I left with a feeling of surging panic taking over, mumbling an unconvinced greeting as I was distancing myself.

After the first encounters, for a while, the figure did not appear at all. It was as if it had sensed that I was becoming aware of its presence, and was starting to play a strange hide-and-seek seduction game. I looked for it over and over again, but there was no trace anywhere. The simple structures resisted piling up on top of each other as they did before; a line, a square, a circle, but nothing resembling their magic accumulation. Time was becoming linear again. The complex structures were no help either; I knew it would be impossible to find it there. Convoluted forms with linear attachments, but lacking the solid underlying structure of the original apparition. The alluring thing I was longing to see was withholding itself from my sight, which made it even more desirable.

The few books which seemed to cover topics related to what I was experiencing had no mention of anything similar. I tried digging out a few collections of fantastic stories, forgotten somewhere in the attic. Nothing of the sort. They were all populated by otherworldly creatures of partially human, partially animal appearance, arousing awe and anxiety. For me it was exactly the opposite: the world was becoming more and more indefinite and terrifying, whereas the marvellous thing, hidden behind its fabric, was slowly taking over anything else.

I took an interest in science as I'd never done before, all in the hope of finding a way to access the mysterious world the strange creature was residing in. For I had decided it must have been something which was alive enticing me through the thick layers of everyday experience. Biology, however, did not help much; none of the registered living forms I came across was even remotely similar. I was hoping that mathematics and physics, with their focus on the abstract and the inorganic, would give me more clues, but the idea of developing some kind of affective relation to any of their objects of study seemed outlandish and, thus, completely unacceptable.

I lost interest in all these fields, as I did in all the other things I used to be excited about. All I wanted to do was walk the streets in search of the beloved creature hiding behind trees and houses. I didn't see it again but finally one day I thought I heard it. At the beginning I was afraid it might just be my imagination, but soon I realised those were not thoughts I could make up. They were coming from without, with the force of a loud sound that fills a room you find yourself stuck in, with no possibility of escape. The sound was first an ongoing, monotonous noise, with nothing in it resembling anything human. I'd never heard it before, and as I started to make it out, nobody else seemed to hear it either. I followed the noise and let myself be guided by its intensity: if I was going the wrong way it was waning and I knew I had to go back, when it was rising to a pitch I knew I was headed in the right direction. I soon realised it had a similar structure to the visual apparitions that had completely changed my life not long before. I was determined not to let it disappear again. Following the complex modulations of the sound I walked the streets I had so often wandered, but none of the places I knew seemed to be where I was being led toward. I left all the familiar areas behind and headed in the direction of the forest, with the same aural indications as an invisible guide. I was becoming more and more impatient; the thought of encountering once again the thing I had so much yearned for filled me with joy and exuberance. When I got to the lake, it seemed the most natural place to be, and the sound confirmed it. I couldn't swim but I stepped in with the confidence of unflinching devotion. The last thing I recall is the blinding light of the afternoon sun.

I can't remember how I got back, or how long it took before I recovered. When I woke up, they told me I had been in bed for a long time, but I had no recollection of it. All I know is that by the first of September there was no sign of it anywhere. I searched every single spot I could imagine; wandered around the streets and the park, and even made it to the lake on an adventurous escape from the now much more restrictive house rules. Gone without a trace. I don't know if it was something they gave me while lying without consciousness that made it impossible for me to see it as I used to, or the thing just decided not to reveal itself anymore. All I know is that ever since I've done nothing other but try to regain that sight.

Vaskelovo. Sunset

ADAM O'RIORDAN

The rain fell in bright patches on the cobbles of Aberlour Street. In reality it was less a street than a passageway, one of those afterthoughts tucked behind the shining windows of the leather goods and jewellery stores on New Bond Street. Nicholas, his ears still ringing with the high, tight tinnitus that came from standing too close to the speakers in the basement nightclub he left only four hours earlier, hurried along the pavement dodging the streams of water that fell from the colourful, well-kept window boxes of the cramped buildings. From the big bay at the front of his office, Rogers looked down to the street below and wondered, not for the first time, where on earth the secretary the agency promised to send over when he called this morning could be. Rogers couldn't stand lateness, it made his gums tingle. Rocco was always telling him in that blowsy

Sicilian way of his *pazienza, pazienza.* He had a vision of his lover in the shower that morning. His lithe, hard body, the pendulous, truncheon-weight of his sex. The vision soothed him and made the lateness momentarily more tolerable. Rogers pinched a fleck of down from the shoulder of his jumper and blew it out onto the air, watching as it lifted and twisted then slowly floated to the floor.

...

Alexei Baskov stepped from the barouche deftly avoiding a muddy puddle that lay like a man-trap beneath him. The late summer light firing the amber strands in his fine moustache as he strode up the stone steps and with considerable vigour swung the polished brass knocker that hung on the door in the shape of a gargoyle. After a moment, Sashenka, the timid Ukrainian maid came to the door. She looked, Alexei thought, like a mouse emerging from its nest after a long hibernation.

'Ah, Alexei Nicoliovic,' she said mournfully, 'come in, come in.'

Dust hung in the silent hallway, the silence accentuated by the grave ticking of an English grandfather clock. Leaning, face-in, against the base of the clock was a small watercolour, *Vaskelovo, Sunset.* Alexei had gifted the painting to Maria's father, Feodor, when he last called. Feodor was an imposing man, a merchant with a series of grain warehouses by the river. Because of his size and thick priest-like beard he was known as *The Black Bear.* It was rumoured he had once flogged a servant to death and that his parents had been registered as serfs on an estate in Azov Guberniya.

'Maria!' Alexei called up joyously, 'I have come to paint you.'

...

'Take a seat,' Rogers said perfunctorily to the sodden young man clutching a copy of the Metro. Nicholas had been using it to shield himself from the rain as he ran to the office from the station. Opening the door, Rogers had been surprised to be met by the young man with the flat-vowels, not the pretty girl, daughter of some City lawyer taking a gap year before starting college, that he had been expecting. Mrs Coombs, the retired Hospital administrator who came in to answer his phones and do some filing for him three days a week, had come into his office at the close of business yesterday to explain that her mother had been taken ill and she had to go to Worthing tomorrow to see her. Mrs Coombs had given Rogers the telephone number of Kensington Secretaries and had assured him they would send over someone suitable.

...

Maria was standing by the window looking down into the garden behind the townhouse. Her hair fell in ringlets at her shoulders. She seemed frozen deep in thought, a sour cast on the corners of her pretty mouth. She had the same gaze, Alexei thought, as he had seen in the portrait of her mother hung in the hallway. Her mother, Frances, an English woman had come to St Petersburg as a governess to a wealthy family of Finnish textile merchants. Within a year of arriving in St Petersburg, Frances had met and married Maria's father, a year later given birth to Maria, and a year later still died, at the age of twenty six, from a haemorrhage of the lung. The dark house was still freighted with her absence.

...

Sellotaped to the desk in the hallway where Nicholas had been prompted to take a seat was a List of Duties for Temporary Staff. It read simply:

1. Answer the telephone cordially with the greeting Rogers Beaux Arts.
2. Establish the name of the caller and the nature of the enquiry.
3. Place the call on hold and relay this information to Mr Rogers.
4. Respond as Mr Rogers directs.

Below this there were three small addenda, the final one in italics:

I. To place calls on hold press *
II. To transfer calls press * followed by 1.
III. *Beaux Arts is pronounced Bow-Ar.*

'Instructions,' Rogers had said pointing to the sheet. 'Lunch at one. Take an hour. Home at five,' before nodding briskly and retreating into his office.

...

As he sat and sketched Maria, the charcoal darkening the page in fine lines that quickly formed her shape, Alexei thought back fondly to earlier in the month when he and Maria had spent the morning walking in the Summer Garden, the excitement of being close to her channelled and intensified by the neat geometrical landscaping of the gardens. As they walked Alexei had pointed out the avenue of sculptures to her and told Maria of their provenance, casually displaying a knowledge of Boratta and Bozzazza. He had talked with great passion to Maria about the previous summer and his time at the Abramtesvo Colony, how the industrialist Savva Ivanovich Mamontov, the little Duke, would hold court amongst the wooden buildings and the fairy tale church. Alexei talked of the excitement he felt being amongst writers and artists and a world of new ideas and how he felt he had been liberated, finally, from the constraints of the Academy. They had stopped at the Tea House, where it had been Maria's turn to talk. She pointed out the statue of Ilya Krylov, the fabulist. She told Alexei the word like a strange bloom flowering from her pretty mouth. She had pointed out the stories carved at the bottom and told Alexei of the occasional walks she would take here in childhood with her father, and the veil of distracted solemnity that hung around them as moved through the park. Always at dusk, her father shrouded in his great black cloak. How on reaching the statue something would surface in him and he would take her on his knee and would retell the fables to her; Fox and Crow, Frog and Bullock, The Peasant and Death, and with the last would scoop her up, folding her in his cloak like a giant crow closing its wing, tickling her ribs as he did through her petticoat. Alexei felt his heart fill with love as she told these stories, as if his own world had been enclosed by a great nebulous glowing net. As the dusk fell and cooled the colours of the summer day to a powder, he walked Maria home and on the doorstep kissed her on the cheek and promised to call again.

...

At 4:58 PM it occurred to Rogers he should make some attempt at conversation with the sodden boy at the desk in the hallway whom he had managed to absentmindedly ignore all day.

'So, Nicholas, where are you from?'

Nicholas explained he was from Manchester.

'I know a chap who made a fortune on the Lowrys.' He spoke the name as one might say *dodgems* or *waltzers*.

'We had a couple of Valettes, rainy city-scapes, went off the boil rather when he returned to France. Vulgar bowls of fruit. You know the stuff. Woeful, really.'

Rogers gave his head a little shake at the decline in Valette's output after leaving the north of England.

'And what brings you to London?'

As Nicholas explained he was a student at Kings, reading English, Rogers noticed a copy of *The Seagull* open on his lap, the plastic library jacket fraying at the edges.

'Like the Russian stuff do you?'

Nicholas smiled.

'Come through, I've got something that might interest you.'

...

'Love,' Alexei said to Vladislav as they sat in the Cafe Dominika playing chess.

'Mmmmm, love,' said Vladislav as he swept Alexei's Bishop from the board with his Queen.

'You want to be careful, you barely know this girl.'

'I know how I feel, Vladislav, I know that much,' Alexei protested.

'Feelings are …' Vladislav paused, his Queen raised at an angle in his hairy hand, 'not always to be trusted.'

He spoke as if translating the phrase from a foreign language.

'Be careful, friend.' Vladislav looked up from the board with a smile. 'Check.'

'I have painted her, Vladislav,' Alexei grinned. 'And such a painting!'

His friend looked across at him pulling his trim beard to a point.

'You have painted her?'

'Beautifully, by a window, in her father's house,' Vladislav nodded. 'As if I were painting with light alone.'

'Oh Alexei, my friend, my dear foolish friend, you are in a bad way.'

Vladislav chuckled and pushed a Rook up the board with his thumb.

'Checkmate.'

…

Rogers' office was filled with paintings cased in various types of elaborate frame, at times three deep against the wall. Some had blankets or loose cotton coverings over them, others were turned face in towards the wall so only the boards on the back were visible, some with the occasional squiggle of an artist's signature and others, those which Rogers wanted to enjoy the thrill of possessing a little while longer before selling on, were placed face out, his own floor level show.

'Contemporary of Korovin and Serov, picked it up in Paris a couple of years ago from Babineaux, an odious little *gascon* with rooms on Rue Guénégaud.'

Rogers looked down at the picture.

'I wasn't certain it would retain its value at auction. Been hoping for private sale. It's been hanging around here since. Can't quite bring myself to get rid of it. Something about her eyes.' Then after a pause. 'Yours for thirty thousand pounds.'

Nicholas smiled and turned out the pockets of his trousers. The cotton lining had dried over the course of the day, the pockets stood crumpled and erect.

'I'm not a huge fan of Russian impressionist portraiture,' Rogers continued. 'Too muscular, all about the male gaze, no invitation to the female at any point,' he said, pulling a small cigar from a leather case he kept in the pocket of his waistcoat.

...

'She is not at home, sir,' Sashenka said feebly to Alexei's feet.

'But I must see her!'

'Please sir, please, she is not at home.' Her plaintive expression urged him to acquiesce to the fiction.

'Sashenka, I must see her.'

Alexei pushed past her into the hallway closing the door on the snow behind him.

'Maria! Maria!' he called up to her. 'Why don't you answer when I come to call?'

Outside snow was falling on the garden. Maria stood by the window looking down.

'Alexei,' she spoke softly, 'you are too much.'

Sick with shock, Alexei looked up at her from the staircase.

'Please go now.'

In the hallway Sashenka touched his elbow. 'A word, please.'

Her voice came to Alexei as if from under a pillow.

'She is a delicate child, she is almost the age her mother was when she ...' Sashenka paused, 'departed'.

She looked up at Alexei. 'Be patient, child'.

Behind her words the ticking clock echoed through the hallway.

...

'Blew his brains out. Hopelessly in love with some girl who refused to marry him, according to Babineaux. Might well be her for all we know.'

Rogers turned the picture back to face the wall.

'You know these Russian types,' he smiled. 'Anyway, you should get going. Very nice to meet you Nicholas. Good luck with your studies and all that.' Rogers offered his hand to shake.

Outside on Aberlour Street the dark cobbles shone as Nicholas picked his way along the pavement, thinking, as he had all day, of the girl he first saw at the library last week. He had watched her looking out of the window on the stairwell. He had seen her again last night at the club, only staying for the final set, eerie minimal techno, in the hope he might get another glimpse of her in the swaying faces. She reminded him of the girl in the painting. He might tell her about it, he thought, if he ran into her tomorrow …

Hi :)

Emma Jane Unsworth

Message
Yesterday 07:32

Hi Jessica, it was good
to meet you last night.
I hope you and your
friends enjoyed the
film and you got home
in time to get packed.
We stayed a bit longer
in the bar but decided
to call it a night around
midnight, probably for
the best as off to the
footie tomorrow. Let
me know if you fancy
a drink when you get
back from Chicago.
Enjoy the wedding.
Best, David

Hi David - good to meet
you too! The film was

ok (did you say you'd seen it?) but there was a ridic bit in an airlock where I laughed and people turned round. Whoops. Still, if you're going to riff on THE seminal space movie you need to do better than Sandra Bullock in her Calvins. Lovely as she is. En route to airport now. Will be in touch when I'm back. Jessica x

Ha, yes I laughed at that bit too. However, I was alone in my mirth. As usual. In fact, that might be the title of my autobiography. Alone In My Mirth. Have a safe flight. Don't go mad in duty free (like I always do). David x

Yesterday 09:18

Trying to resist the urge to buy lipgloss… Jx

I think you can probably justify that as a head-bridesmaid cost. Dx

How many Toblerones is too many Toblerones? X

The giant ones? I'd say
five or six. X

GET THEE BEHIND
ME. X

Yesterday 12:41

Landed safe! I'm just
rehearsing my speech
now, arg! Going to have
a bit of Dutch courage.
Well, Italian (Prosecco).
Hope you're having a
lovely day. Jessica x

PS Here's me in my
dress looking nervous!
And slightly like Bet
Lynch.

Fierce dress. How did
it go? Did you dance
with the best man, as is
tradition? Dx

Hellooooo! Bit drunk
now! But it wqent SO
WELL. People even

laughed in the right
places, which was nice.
Phewww

Are you

Seen too soon! Are you
having a god Saturday?
Jx

Sent too soon! Damn
you autocorrect! Xx

Good! GOD. Xxx

Sorry for all the
messages, David - I
know we've only
just met! I blame the
excitement! It's not
every day your oldest
friend gets married. I'm
not sure you're even
getting these because
it keeps going to green
not blue. Or does that
always happen when
you're abroad? I can't
remember. Anyway,
rambling! Maybe we
should swap email
addresses to keep
talking, rather than
these crazily long
expensive texts. I am
jessicaforestcat@
hotmail.com because
i used to have a forest
cat - have you seen

them? They're amazing
and they're the only
cats that can get down
trees, I'll show you
some pics sometime.
He was called Simon
and he died last year
but he was living with
my parents by then
anyway. I still miss him,
Anyway! X

PS I know it's not
cool to have a hotmail
account and I should
be on gmail by now
but you know when
it just feels like it'll be
the biggest ballache
to transfer all your
contacts over etc etc?
X

PPS I hope you're
having a nice afternoon
- I'm presuming it is
afternoon there by
now?

PPPS You probably
have a wife anyway
don't you! It wouldn't
be the first time some
tosser has led me on.

PPPPS That was sort
of a joke. I just tried
to call you but it went
straight to voicemail

so I'm thinking you're
out of reception or had
enough of me going on.
Anyway, have a nice
life. X

Today 10:15

Hi David. Oh god, really
sorry about all those
messages last night. I
understand if you don't
want to meet up now
or if you just think I'm a
weirdo or psychopath.
Wishing you all the very
best, Jessica.

Hi David, not sure
if my last message
got through but I just
wanted to say again
how sorry I am about
all those messages.
Jessica.

Hi Nic, can I forward
you some texts I sent
to this new bloke after
one too many at Jen's
wedding? I'm freaking
out because I think I
might have sounded
like a total psycho. Also
am so hungover I want
to die. If I fwd them to
you now can you call
me when you've read
them and tell me what
you think? There's no

way they can tell when
you've forwarded their
texts, is there? Also
I sent him one really
early on in our comms
that said 'get thee
behind me' in capitals
and I'm worried he
didn't know the Satan
reference and thought I
was being prematurely
sexual? Oh god. Can
I send you that one
too? Jx

Arg sorry David, that
last text was meant for
my friend. Okay, I'm
really going to leave this
now because I feel like
I've completely fucked
up. I don't blame you
for ignoring me. It
was nice to meet you.
Jessica.

Jessica, sorry I've just
got up and seen these,
I had a bit of a lie-in
as I had quite a few
last night myself and I
left my phone at home
when I went to football
and it had run out of
battery by the time I got
back. Just seen these
now. Wow. Weddings
are lethal, eh. Don't
worry. Well done on the

speech. Drink some
water. And FYI I don't
have a wife. David x

David - hi. Yep, this
one burns. I'm beyond
embarrassed. Thanks
for being nice. X

I must admit I had to
laugh at the one meant
for your friend. I've
done something similar
with a work email
before. Mortifying. X

Oh yeah thanks for
reminding me about
that one. I'd forgotten
about it, and hadn't
been shrivelling into a
ball of remorse about it
ALL morning. Nope, not
at all. X

Haha. Have you taken
some ibuprofen? X

A whole packet. I'd
like to leave my books
to my nephew, my
jewellery to the Cats'
Protection League,
and my debt to Gary
Barlow. X

My sister died from an
ibuprofen overdose.

No wait, it wasn't my
sister. It was my wife.

I hate you.

That's really sick, by
the way.

Sorry, couldn't resist.

Stop torturing me! I'm
in no state to defend
myself.

Sorry. Anyway, have to
go. I'm off out to meet
my friend for Sunday
lunch. X

Okay - have a lovely
time. I'm meeting
a friend for dinner
shortly too. (I won't be
drinking.) X

Famous last words ;) Is
it your friend who got
married? X

No, old pal from when
I used to live in the
States. X

Hi Jessica, hope you had a nice meal with your old pal. I had a really fantastic meal at this new place called Mr Smithy's that's just opened in the Northern Quarter and specialises in chops. Perfect Sunday fodder. Had a fair bit of red wine, but I'm hoping I don't regret this tomorrow! I thought I'd take you up on your email offer so we could chat a bit more while you're still over there. I hope your hangover has gone and you're feeling better. I wanted to say that I was secretly pleased to see all those messages from you this morning because it implied you were interested, and in all honesty I've been thinking about you a lot, more than I usually would after just meeting someone for half an hour in a bar on a Friday night. I hope this doesn't sound presumptuous or creepy, but I feel like there's a connection between us that I haven't felt for a long time. Did you say you were over there for a week? Do you want to plan a date for when you get back?
Take care,
David x
Sent from my iPad

Hi David,
Just outside having a fag between courses! Aw, this is lovely, thank you - and I do know what you mean, it's weird but I've been thinking about you a lot, too. And not just out of embarrassment :) I feel strangely like I know you more than I should at this stage. That's good, isn't it! Gotta get back inside but more later, and yes let's plan a date - next weekend maybe?
Jx
Sent from my Android

Hi Jessica,
Is it a male or female old pal? I probably shouldn't even ask that and you don't have to answer, but I guess I just wanted to know if you're on a date, just so I know where I stand.
Dx
Sent from my iPad

Not a date, no. Female friend. Lol. X
Sent from my Android

Glad about that. You looked hot in that dress, by the way. It did things to me.
Sent from my iPad

Xxxxxx
Sent from my Android

Off to bed now to think about you in your dress.
Sent from my iPad

Easy, tiger. Sweet dreams.
Sent from my Android

Grrrrll
Sent from my iPad

Haha okay - how much red wine did you have? Not that I can talk obvs. Maybe remove your device sign-off tho for future flirty conversations. Nothing undermines a sext quite like the suffix 'sent from my iPad'. I mean, iPads might be modern design classics but they're hardy erotic. Xx
Sent from my Android

Well now I just feel stupid. Sorry.

I was joking! God, okay. Want to chat on the phone tomorrow?
Sent from my Android

Not sure. Are phones 'erotic' enough for you?
David.
Sent from my iPad

I'll call you at 11am, your time. Dx
Sent from my iPad

I'll answer. Jx
Sent from my Android

ABOUT THE AUTHORS

AL AND AL are film makers, writers and visual artists who investigate the shaping forces of fantasy and reality. Since 2001 the duo have created an award winning body of films which have been exhibited internationally. In 2010 AL and AL began working on an epic sci-fi odyssey, collaborating with physicist Brian Greene, composer Philip Glass and nano-biophysicist Bart Hoogenboom. AL and AL are currently in pre-production on their debut theatrical feature film, *The Creator.*

JUDITH BARRY is an artist and writer whose work crosses a number of disciplines: performance, installation, sculpture, architecture, photography and new media. She has exhibited internationally at such venues as the Berlin Biennale, Venice Biennale(s) of Art/Architecture, Sharjah Biennial, Sao Paolo Biennale, Nagoya Biennale, Carnegie International, Whitney Biennale, and the Sydney Biennale, among others. Her work is included in the collection of MOMA, NYC; Whitney Museum, NYC; Generali Foundation, Vienna; MCA, San Diego; Pompidou Centre, Paris; Le Caixa, Barcelona; MACBA, Barcelona; FNAC, Paris; Goetz collection, Munich; Frac Lorraine, Metz; and CIFO, Miami, among others.

DECLAN CLARKE is an artist whose films intertwine personal subjectivity and action with grand narratives and explorations of the historical edifices of power. They have recently been included in the Tromsø International Film Festival in 2014; Cinéphémère, Jardin Des Tuilieries, FIAC, Paris; and FIDMarseille – Marseille's International Film Festival, both 2013.

DOUGLAS COUPLAND is a Canadian novelist, visual artist and designer. His first novel in 1991 was *Generation X: Tales for an Accelerated Culture.* He has published thirteen novels, a collection of short stories, seven nonfiction books, and a number of dramatic works and screenplays for film and television. Coupland's novels and visual work synthesise high and low culture, web technology, religion, and changes in human existence caused by modern technologies.

ANDREW DURBIN is the author of *Mature Themes* (2014). A contributing editor of *Mousse*, his work has appeared in *Artforum, Boston Review, Flash Art, Triple Canopy,* and elsewhere. He co-edits the publisher Wonder and curates the talks series at the Poetry Project. He lives in New York.

IRINA GHEORGHE is an artist from Bucharest, Romania. Recently she published *A Short History of the Vague*, exploring topics such as ambiguity and dissimulation and is currently researching the overspill of the exact sciences into the occult which was exhibited in a project for Salonul de Proiecte, MNAC (Bucharest, RO). Irina co-founded the artist duo The Bureau of Melodramatic Research in 2009 which investigates how elements of melodrama (emotion, gender and the body) shape contemporary society and the new working place.

OMAR KHOLEIF is a writer, curator and editor. He has authored or edited nearly twenty books including, *You Are Here: Art After the Internet, Virgin with a Memory: The Exhibition-Tie In, Jeddah Childhood circa 1994, Before History and Two Days After Forever: A Reader on the Choreography of Time.*

CHRIS MCCORMACK is a writer and editor based in London. He is currently Assistant Editor at *Art Monthly* and Commissioning Editor – *ON&BY* for MIT Press and Whitechapel Gallery, London.

ADAM O'RIORDAN was born in Manchester in 1982 and read English at Oxford University. In 2008, O'Riordan became the youngest Poet-in-Residence at The Wordsworth Trust, the Centre for British Romanticism. His first collection *In the Flesh* (Chatto and Windus) won a Somerset Maugham Award in 2011. He is Lecturer in Poetry Writing at the Writing School at Manchester Metropolitan University.

SARAH PERKS is a curator, film programmer and producer, with over ten years experience of working in contemporary visual art and independent film. She is a specialist in artist feature film, performance and participatory art. In 2011, Sarah set up HOME Artist Film (then Cornerhouse Artist Film) as a means of investigating new methods for the production, distribution and exhibition of artist feature film. She is also Professor of Visual Arts at Manchester School of Art, part of Manchester Metropolitan University.

KATIE POPPERWELL is a writer and producer. Her work is informed by her background in critical and cultural theory with an emphasis on the politics of identity. She lives in Old Trafford with her partner and eleven-year old son.

GREG THORPE is a writer, journalist, DJ, club promoter, and arts event co-ordinator. He has written for *City Life, Time Out, The Big Issue, Creative Tourist, Manchester Evening News, Northern Soul* and has been a writer in residence for Islington Mill and Manchester Central Library. For the last seven years he has written the *Manhattanchester* blog. He is a graduate of the University of Manchester and The Writing School at MMU.

JESSEY TSANG is a filmmaker and video-maker. Her early works are short pieces based on the lives of herself and the people around her, such as *Jeffven & Jordy* (2001) and *Chan Sau Chun* (2001), both co-directed with Eric Hui Chungyin and both winning prizes at the Hong Kong Independent Short Film and Video Awards (IFVA). In 2008, Tsang released her first feature, *Lovers on the Road* (2008), the story of a Hong Kong woman's life in the city of Beijing, which won the Best Feature award at the 2009 South Taiwan Film and Video Festival. Her second feature, *Big Blue Lake* (2011), set in the Hou Chung area of Sai Kung where she grew up, won several awards in Hong Kong and internationally, such as the Jury Prix at the Shanghai International Film Festival, Best New Director at the Hong Kong Film Awards and New Artist Award by the Hong Kong Art Development Council.

LYNNE TILLMAN is a novelist, short story writer, and critic. Her novel *American Genius, A Comedy* was cited as one of the best books of the Millennium (so far) by *The Millions.* Her other novels are *Haunted Houses, Motion Sickness, Cast In Doubt,* and *No Lease On Life,* a finalist for the National Book Critics Circle Award in fiction and a *New York Times* Notable Book of the Year. Her fourth collection of stories, *Someday This Will Be Funny,* was published in April 2011 by Red Lemonade Press. Her other story collections are *This Is Not It,* stories and novellas written in response to the work of 22 contemporary artists; *The Madame Realism Complex;* and *Absence Makes The Heart.* She has published four nonfiction books: *The Broad Picture, an essay collection* (1997); *The Velvet Years: Warhol's Factory 1965-67, based on photographs by Stephen Shore* (1995); *Bookstore: The Life And Times Of Jeannette Watson And Books & Co.* Most recently, her second essay collection *What Would Lynne Tillman Do?* was a finalist for the 2014 National Book Critics Circle Award in Criticism.

EMMA JANE UNSWORTH'S first novel *Hungry, the Stars and Everything* (2011) won a Betty Trask Award from the Society of Authors and was shortlisted for the Portico Prize 2012. Her short story *I Arrive First* was included in *The Best British Short Stories 2012.* She has worked as a journalist, a columnist for *The Big Issue,* and a barmaid. Her second novel *Animals* was published by Canongate in May 2014. She is writing a third novel, as well as the screenplay of *Animals,* which has been optioned by BAFTA-nominated producer Sarah Brocklehurst and awarded development funding by the BFI.

JASON WOOD is Artistic Director of Film at HOME. He is also the author of multiple books on cinema, most recently, *Last Words: Considering Contemporary Cinema* (2014).

Transactions of Desire
Edited by Omar Kholeif & Sarah Perks

First published in the United Kingdom in 2015 by:
HOME Publications

On the occasion of the exhibition:
The Heart is Deceitful Above All Things
Sat 23rd May – Sun 26th July 2015

HOME
2 Tony Wilson Place
First Street, Manchester
M15 4FN, United Kingdom
www.homemcr.org

ISBN 978-0-9929524-3-3

Authors:
AL and AL, Judith Barry, Declan Clarke, Douglas Coupland, Andrew Durbin, Irina Gheorghe, Omar Kholeif, Chris McCormack, Adam O'Riordan. Sarah Perks, Katie Popperwell, Greg Thorpe, Jessey Tsang, Lynne Tillman, Emma Jane Unsworth and Jason Wood.

Editors:
Omar Kholeif & Sarah Perks

Producer:
Bren O'Callaghan

Design and Art Direction:
Minute Works

Cover illustration:
Jai Redman

Distributed worldwide by:
Cornerhouse Publications
www.cornerhousepublications.org

HOME

MANCHESTER
SCHOOL OF ART